KATIE'S BABY-SITTING JOB

Martha Tolles

AN
APPLE®
PAPERBACK

SCHOLASTIC INC.
New York Toronto London Auckland Sydney

To our five sons and their sister.

**Also by Martha Tolles,
available from Apple:**

Who's Reading Darci's Diary?

Coming soon:
Darci and the Dance Contest

Library of Congress Cataloging in Publication Data
Tolles, Martha.
Katie's babysitting job.

Summary: When several pieces of valuable jewelry disappeared during Katie's first babysitting job, she finds that she must discover the explanation to clear her own name.
[1. Baby sitters—Fiction. 2. Mystery and detective stories] I. Title.
PZ7.T5745Kat 1985   [Fic]   85-10780

ISBN 0-590-40724-4

12 11 10 9 8 7 6 5 4 3 2   7 8 9/8 0/9

Printed in the U.S.A.   11

Contents

New Neighbors

Katie Hart looked around the crowded cafeteria of Hemsted School. She had great news that she could hardly wait to tell her friend, Sarah Lou. The bright, sunny room was swarming with seventh and eighth graders — some of them were lined up at the lunch counter, others were carrying trays of hot, steaming food to the long tables where their friends were waiting.

Most of the seats filled before Katie spotted Sarah Lou's long blond ponytail and rushed across the room to her friend.

"Sarah Lou!" she exclaimed. "Guess what?" Katie plopped down on the chair her friend had saved for her, and dropped her lunch bag on the table.

"Hi Katie!" Sarah Lou looked up from the wrinkled pages of an old Christmas catalog she'd been studying lately for gift ideas. "What's up? It must be good, I'd guess."

Katie beamed. "It is. You know those new people in our neighborhood?"

Sarah Lou made a face. "You don't mean that new girl, Michelle, do you?" Sarah Lou opened her lunch bag and pulled out some carrot sticks.

"Well, not exactly." Katie glanced around at the other kids at their table. They were mostly eighth graders and a few other seventh graders she didn't really know very well. But she lowered her voice anyway and leaned confidentially toward Sarah Lou. "I was talking about the other new family, the Stellans. Mom told me last night that they have a three-year-old girl and she heard Mrs. Stellan is asking around about baby-sitters. I'm going to go see her right after school today." Katie opened her lunch bag, but she was too excited to begin eating.

"Katie, how terrific! Now you can get a baby-sitting job, too, just like Jody and me."

"Oh, I hope I can." Katie had wanted a baby-sitting job for so long. But Mom and Dad insisted it had to be right in the neighborhood, and there just weren't any little kids on Apple Street who needed sitters — until now, anyway.

"I just hope nobody else in the neighborhood wants the job," Katie added in a low voice, "like that Michelle, for instance. She lives right behind the Stellans and her little sister probably plays with their little girl."

"E-w-w-w!" Sarah Lou squealed and cast a quick

look around the crowded cafeteria. "Maybe she won't want it. Besides, you can tell Mrs. Stellan you've had a lot of experience taking care of your brother Jamie. And now you have a new baby brother, too."

"True." Katie had had plenty of experience with Jamie, all right. Once he'd brushed red paint all over himself, another time he'd put bubble gum in her hair, and she'd never forget the time he'd locked her in the basement for a whole afternoon.

Katie happened to look up just then and saw a dark-haired girl approaching. "Sarah Lou," she whispered. "Michelle's coming this way." Sure enough, she was heading toward them. Michelle's dark bangs hung down almost to her eyes and she seemed to be looking straight at them.

Sarah Lou glanced around, then quickly slid her chair closer to Katie. "Do you suppose she wants to sit with us?"

Katie got ready to smile just in case, and was about to say hello, when Michelle's glance moved on to someone behind them. "Wait, you guys," she called out, and hurried over to two seventh grade boys who were just leaving the cafeteria. One was Will Madison, who lived next door to Katie. She used to think he was sort of a pest, but lately she had been thinking Will was pretty much okay and wondering how he felt about her.

"Look at that," Sarah Lou whispered. "She's always talking to the boys." Sarah Lou began to nibble on a cookie.

"I know," Katie agreed. "That's just the way she is whenever she comes over to our street. It would've been great having another girl in the neighborhood, but she's so unfriendly."

"Listen, Katie," Sarah Lou said. "Don't worry about Michelle. Think about all the money you're going to make baby-sitting. Guess what I might give my mom for Christmas?" Sarah Lou shook back her blond ponytail proudly.

Katie tried to forget about Michelle and think about Sarah Lou's mother. "Can't guess."

"There's this neat perfume on sale at the drug store now. It's called, listen to this, Sinsation. M-m-m-m, what a smell!" Sarah Lou rolled her eyes ecstatically. "It's almost eight dollars, but it's a big bottle."

"That sounds super," Katie agreed. It was way more than she could get for her mother right now.

"On Saturday Jody and I are going down to the mall to get more ideas for Christmas gifts. Do you want to come, too?" Sarah Lou asked.

Katie felt a little stab of envy. Her friends made plans without her. They went shopping and wrote out Christmas lists because they had baby-sitting jobs. "I don't have enough money saved yet," she admitted. Her small allowance kept going for hair

4

bands, or barrettes, or that yummy new ice cream in the mall. It was so hard to save. She'd just have to get this job. She'd hurry home this afternoon and get right down to the Stellans' before anyone else did.

As soon as classes ended Katie grabbed her jacket and backpack and rushed out to the parking lot to wait for her older brother. Dick was in high school and he drove to school almost every day. Please, come soon, Katie prayed. She hoisted her backpack on her shoulders impatiently as buses loaded with students began to pull out of the parking lot and carloads of kids moved briskly past her. She waved good-bye to some friends boarding a bus, and watched Michelle getting on the bus that went out to Apple Street. Oh, where was Dick anyway? She just hoped he wasn't having car trouble again.

Finally, the old red car, with Dick at the wheel, bumped into the parking lot. His brown hair tumbled onto his forehead as usual, and as usual, next to him were his friends from Apple Street — Miller who was very tall and skinny, and Bob who played football. As Katie raced toward them a voice called, "Wait Dick! I'm coming, too." It was Will Madison, running toward them from the ball field. Katie slid over to make room for him. Will, with his blue eyes and bright red hair, always looked so cheerful. No wonder Michelle wanted to talk to him. Thinking of Michelle and how she must be halfway home by now, made Katie eager to get going. But the car wasn't moving and Dick was bent over the steering wheel, listening to the engine.

"I hope you don't have car trouble," Katie said anxiously. "I'm in a big hurry today."

"Yeah, me, too," Will said. "I have to get my papers ready soon."

Lucky Will, he had a paper route and was making money. Well, maybe she'd have a job today, too.

Dick straightened up and the car began to roll forward. "Everything's okay," he said over his shoulder and steered the car out of the parking lot.

"Want to help me with my papers, Katie?" Will poked her with his elbow and grinned at her.

"Oh, sure." Katie laughed, but then she wondered, Did he really mean that? She stole another quick look at him. She wouldn't mind helping him.

As they drove along, Katie kept worrying about how to approach Mrs. Stellan, while the guys talked about football and what they'd do when they got home. If only she could get the job and baby-sit every weekend between now and Christmas. Think of the money she could make and the great gifts she could buy. How she hoped Michelle wouldn't want the job, too.

At last they were turning onto Apple Street — wide, quiet, and tree-lined. As they neared home Katie saw Jamie out front on his bike, and that gave her a sudden terrific idea. As soon as Dick pulled up in front of their house, she climbed out of the car.

"Jamie," she shouted. "Wait — don't go." He was about to shove off down the sidewalk. "I want to ask you something."

Katie ran down the sidewalk toward her brother. "Jamie, listen, would you walk down the street with me now to meet the new neighbors, the Stellans?"

"Why?" Jamie scowled. "What for? Are you afraid to go by yourself?" He grinned at Katie.

"Look, just let me put my books in the house. I'll make a deal with you."

"Well, maybe." Jamie flopped down on the grass. "It better be good, though."

Katie threw her backpack down in the front hall. "Mom, I'm home," she called up the stairs, where her mother would be busy with the baby, and ran back outside.

Next door Will was throwing a football around with Miller and Bob. Unfortunately, Jamie was now watching them with interest. Katie hurried toward him.

"Jamie, I'll make you a deal." Katie tried to get his attention. "I really need your help." She could

7

promise him she'd be able to buy him a nice Christmas present, but the holidays would seem so far away to Jamie. "If you'll come with me, I'll give you my dessert tonight. It'll be chocolate pudding, too."

Jamie looked at her with sudden interest. "Oh, yeah? How do you know?"

"I'll make it, that's how. Mom will be glad to have me fix the dessert. So, please, Jamie, will you come? Now? Right now?" It would look so much better if Jamie were with her. That would show Mrs. Stellan that Katie was used to kids, knew how to handle them.

Jamie threw a last, regretful glance at the boys on Will's lawn. "Okay, Katie — for you — and lots of chocolate pudding. But it better not have lumps."

"Good. Come on. Let's go. No lumps, I promise." As they crossed the street Katie looked down toward the Stellans' house. The trees lining the sidewalk were almost bare, and everywhere there were scatterings of brown and yellow leaves. Jamie kicked at them as they walked along. The Stellans' house up ahead was a small, white, one-story bungalow with green shutters —just the right size for a mother, a father, and a little girl, with one baby-sitter, Katie thought.

"Hurry, Jamie," she urged.

"Okay, okay," Jamie grumbled. "But I still don't

get it. Why did you ask me to walk down here with you? I've been walking down this street by myself for years."

"Oh, sure, *years*," Katie scoffed at her six-year-old brother. "It'll look . . . uh . . . friendlier, Jamie. Don't you see?" She wished he would stop frowning. How could she impress Mrs. Stellan if Jamie looked as if he were in misery?

"I just want to meet Mrs. Stellan. You see, she has a little girl and — "

Jamie stopped short. "Yuck! I don't want to play with any little girl. Is that why you want me to go?" He scowled horribly.

"No, no," Katie replied hastily. "I want to try to get a job baby-sitting. I just thought it would . . . uh . . . look good if you came, too." It seemed best not to tell Jamie he was her living example of someone she could take care of. "You know, we're greeting the new neighbors and all that. Besides, remember the chocolate pudding."

"Oh, all right." Jamie started walking again, shuffling through the leaves. "But I'm not staying long."

"You don't have to stay long," Katie assured him, as they turned up the front walk of the Stellans' house. "All you have to do is stand there and be polite." Katie glanced at her brother — mussed up brown hair, old red jacket, and worn jeans.

She wished he looked better. Maybe it had been a mistake to bring him. She quickly smoothed her own long brown hair and hoped she looked okay, but it was too late to worry now. They were climbing the front steps. Katie's palms felt damp. What should she say?

The Phone Call

For a full minute Katie stared at the Stellans' front door, nervously pushing her hair behind her ears. When Jamie started backing away toward the steps, she quickly rang the doorbell.

Immediately a dog barked inside the house and soon they heard a little girl's voice behind the front door. "Mommy, somebody's here."

"Oh, no," Jamie groaned. "Let's go home."

"Sh-h-h-h, quiet!" Katie commanded. "You promised, remember?" When the front door opened, a slender woman, a little girl, and a small black dog looked out at them.

"Hello," Katie said quickly. "Are you Mrs. Stellan? I'm Katie Hart from up the street. And this is my brother, Jamie."

"Why, how nice to meet you. Katie and Jamie, this is my daughter, Annie, and this is our dog, Scratch." Mrs. Stellan was smiling at them. So far so good, Katie thought.

"Hi, Annie," Katie said in her friendliest voice.

Looking down at the eager blond-haired little girl, Katie wished she'd reminded Jamie to say hello.

"Hi-i-i-i." The little girl moved toward Jamie and beamed up at him. "You want to play?"

Katie threw her brother a you-be-nice-or-I'll-get-you-later look.

"Hi," Jamie said unwillingly, ignoring Annie.

"Which house do you two live in?" Mrs. Stellan asked.

"The brown shingled one on the other side of the street." Katie waved in the direction of her house. "My mom wants to meet you soon, too." Katie was pretty sure her mom had said something like that.

"That would be nice." Mrs. Stellan opened the door wider. "Would you like to come in?"

Katie was sure Jamie wouldn't want to. He was looking down at Annie as if she were a species of spider. "I don't think we better today. I just wanted to ask . . . well, you see, my mom told me about your moving in and about your little girl." Katie wondered if Annie would be easier to take care of than Jamie. She looked like a quiet little girl, with those big thoughtful blue eyes.

"So, I thought you might need a baby-sitter sometime. I'm in seventh grade and I've taken care of Jamie lots of times." She wished she could tell Mrs. Stellan just how challenging it was to take care of Jamie, but she decided not to. "I have friends my age who baby-sit and — "

"I'm no baby," Jamie said loudly. "I don't need anyone to take care of me." He punched Katie in the side.

"Jamie!" Katie frowned hard at him.

Mrs. Stellan smiled again. She had shiny white teeth and brown eyes that seemed to be laughing, for sure. Katie noticed for the first time that Mrs. Stellan looked dressed to go out. She was wearing a silk print dress, high-heeled shoes, and red and gold earrings with a matching bracelet.

"Are you going somewhere tonight?" Katie blurted out, then wondered if she should have asked. "I mean, maybe you need a sitter right away?"

"No, thank you," Mrs. Stellan said. "Tonight Annie is invited to go, too."

"Well, maybe you'd want me sometime. I also help my mom take care of my baby brother, Peter." Katie hurried on. "My mom stays home a lot with him so she'd be there if I needed help or anything." Oh, maybe she shouldn't have said that about needing help. Katie glanced down at the little black dog Jamie was enthusiastically petting. "I could take care of Scratch, too, if you wanted me to, feed him and all that."

Mrs. Stellan nodded. "Those are good ideas, Katie. I'll keep you in mind. But now Annie and I better hustle or we'll be late." Mrs. Stellan called to Scratch and started to close the door. "Thank you for coming by," she said.

"Thank you, Mrs. Stellan. Good-bye, Annie."

Annie kept peeking around the closing door. "Bye . . . bye," she called to Jamie.

Katie and Jamie started down the front walk together.

"Yuck! Remember, I'm not playing with her. Her dog might be okay, though."

"They're all okay, if you ask me," Katie said.

"I hope, oh, how I hope." Mrs. Stellan had said she would keep Katie in mind. Katie just hoped she wouldn't keep Michelle in mind, too.

Jamie pointed excitedly up the street. "Look, there's Will. I'm going to help him with his newspapers." Will was bent over a stack of newspapers on the sidewalk in front of his house. "Hey, Will," Jamie bellowed, "can I help fold your papers?"

Will looked up and waved him on. Bob and Miller were gone now, but someone else was there, talking and laughing with Will.

It was Michelle. Katie slowed up. Should she go over and speak to her? But of course . . . she must. Katie decided she would try again to be friendly. Maybe she hadn't really given Michelle a chance, and it would be so good to have a friend nearby.

"Hi," Katie called out as she approached them.

14

Will looked up from the paper he was folding and grinned in her direction. Michelle glanced at her, too, but didn't say anything. She just stood there, watching Will and Jamie folding papers.

"Hello, Michelle," Katie said as she reached the group.

"Hi," Michelle answered. "Have you been taking a walk with your brother?" Michelle glanced down the street toward the Stellans' house.

"Uh, sort of," Katie said. "You could call it that." She wondered if Michelle had seen her at Mrs. Stellan's door.

Jamie looked up from the newspaper he was folding. "We had to go see a dumb little girl," he said loudly.

Katie groaned inside. She felt like shaking him. Why couldn't he keep from blabbing? "Had to meet our new neighbors," Katie explained quickly.

"Annie Stellan? Sure, I know them. My sister, Cheri, plays with Annie."

Michelle had the edge, no doubt about it. If she wanted a baby-sitting job at the Stellans', she'd probably get it. Katie felt discouraged.

"Well, that's it," Will said, stuffing the last of the newspapers into the bags on his bike. "Guess I'm ready to roll."

"I have to go, too," Michelle said quickly. "Goodbye." She smiled but seemed to be looking mainly at Will; then she started off down the street. That was the way things always seemed to work out with Michelle — cool and unfriendly.

"See you kids later." Will grinned at Katie and Jamie.

"See you," Katie said, and started slowly toward her house. Things didn't look too hopeful. Maybe she should try to get a paper route like Will's. But she knew she'd have to wait for months before a route opened up, and then it might be on the other side of town. She had to think of some way to get Mrs. Stellan to hire her.

By the next afternoon Katie had a plan to impress Mrs. Stellan. She told Mom she'd like to take Peter for a walk. Mom agreed the fresh air would be good for Peter, and a little while later Katie was pushing the Harts' old baby carriage down Apple Street. Maybe Mrs. Stellan would look out her window and see her and think, My, that Katie Hart would make a good baby-sitter. Even if Mrs. Stellan did hire Michelle, perhaps there'd be times when Michelle wasn't free.

When Katie came to the Stellans' she stopped in front of the house and adjusted Peter's covers for a long time. If only Mrs. Stellan would come out. Or Annie. They would like Peter, Katie was sure. He would smile and make funny little laughing noises when they talked to him. With his blue knitted cap poking above the blue and white quilt, he looked like a big doll. She remembered how, before he was born, she'd hoped he would be a girl. But now, somehow that didn't matter.

At the corner of Apple Street Katie turned and pushed the carriage back past the Stellans' house. She stopped and tucked the quilt around Peter again, although he was asleep now and hadn't moved. No one came out of the Stellans' house and she finally went home.

Katie wanted to walk Peter past the Stellan house again the next afternoon. But Mom said he had a little fever and it wouldn't be good for him to go out. Katie was really disappointed. She had planned on this and she felt let down. She wanted to show Mrs. Stellan how good she was at taking care of a younger child. Maybe Jamie would help her again. She went out front where he was playing in a pile of leaves on the lawn.

"Jamie," she hurried over to him. "How about taking a ride in your wagon down the street? I'll pull you."

"What do you want to do that for?" Jamie regarded her with suspicion. "Besides, my wagon's broken." He kicked a huge cloud of leaves into the air.

So that wouldn't work. As she walked slowly back toward the house, she had the solution. She'd take the buggy anyway, the empty buggy, and put a stuffed toy in it and cover it with a blanket. "Ha-ha," she laughed out loud. It would work if no one came out of the house.

"What's so funny?" Jamie called out.

"Oh, nothing," she said. Katie looked up and down Apple Street quickly. None of the guys were around, but she'd have to get Jamie out of the front yard, too. "Jamie, why don't you come inside and watch TV? There's nothing going on out here."

Jamie took a look up and down the street. "Yeah, you're right." He gave the pile of leaves a last kick and came toward her.

With Jamie watching TV and Mom busy rocking Peter, the coast would be clear! Katie hurried to get ready.

In a few minutes she was wheeling a stuffed bear with a blue cap on its head down Apple Street. It was tucked under Peter's blue and white quilt and from a distance no one would think it wasn't a baby. Katie walked rapidly; she didn't want to meet *anyone*. She passed the Stellans' house just fast enough so that someone looking out the window and catching a glimpse of her would think: That Katie Hart, she really cares about kids.

Then as she was coming back up the street she saw Will pedaling toward her on his bike. What rotten luck! He was through with his paper route early! She hurried across the street toward her driveway, pretending she hadn't seen him.

"How's Peter?" Will called, coming closer. If he found out she was wheeling a teddy bear, he'd tease her forever! And he might tell everyone!

Katie put her finger to her lips so Will would think Peter was asleep in the carriage, and then she practically ran down the driveway, bouncing the buggy as she went. She darted around the corner of the house, swooped up the quilt and the bear, and rushed inside. Safe in the kitchen, she leaned against the door, gasping for breath. Boy, was that ever close. She wasn't going to try that again. Maybe she'd impressed Mrs. Stellan enough for now. She'd just wait, see how things went.

That night when Katie was just sitting down to dinner with her family, the phone rang. "I'll answer it," she offered, getting up from the table. "Maybe it's Sarah Lou."

When Katie picked up the phone out in the hall, a voice said, "Katie, this is Mrs. Stellan. Could you baby-sit for us on Saturday night?" Just like that, it had happened!

Could she! Would she! Her first job . . . her first pay! "Oh yes, yes. I could!" she managed to say. Mrs. Stellan talked on about how pleased Annie would be, but Katie was in such a happy daze she hardly heard. Then Mrs. Stellan was saying, "See you then."

Katie hung up and rushed back to the dining room. "Mom, Dad, I've got it! I've got it!"

"What's she got?" Jamie asked, his mouth full of mashed potatoes. "A bad cold or something?" He grinned.

"I'd say it's something good." Dad gave Katie an amused look through his dark framed glasses.

"Oh, it is, Dad. Guess what it is."

"Well, let's see." Mom set down the salad bowl and pushed back her dark hair thoughtfully. Then she smiled at Katie. "Maybe I can figure it out."

"That was Mrs. Stellan," Katie beamed, "and she wants me to baby-sit this Saturday night. Me! Think of the money I'll make!"

Dick looked up from his plate heaped with food. "Good for you — Katie, the baby-sitter."

"Is that all? Taking care of a baby!" Jamie said. "I'd rather take care of the dog."

But Katie didn't care. She was already starting back to the phone. "I've got to call Sarah Lou and tell her the news."

Saturday Night

At three o'clock Saturday afternoon Katie started getting dressed to go to the Stellans'. She picked out a red sweater (she'd heard that little kids liked red) and a new pair of jeans. Then she put on her sneakers so she could get around fast if she had to. Katie looked in the mirror and gave her hair a quick brush . . . long brown hair, big hazel eyes. Did she look as pretty as Michelle? She hoped she at least looked like someone who could handle things. Finally, she picked up her shoulder bag and went out into the hall, ready for her first real job.

"Bye, Mom." Katie waved. Mom, dressed in brown wool slacks and a light-colored blouse, was sitting in the big wooden rocking chair in her bedroom. Peter, wrapped in a bright yellow blanket and tucked in her arms, was staring up into her face as she rocked him. This was his fussy time of day when he wanted to be held, but he looked content with Mom holding him.

"Good-bye, Katie. Call me if you have any problems. Don't forget now, dear. We'll be right here."

"Sure, Mom. But I won't have to. Annie looks like a good little kid."

"Well, just in case." Mom lifted Peter up on her shoulder and began to rub his back. He wobbled his little head around as if he was trying to get a good look at Mom's ear, or maybe the small gold earring in her ear.

"You know me, Mom. Look at all the times I've taken care of Jamie." Katie hurried down the stairs, grabbed her jacket from the hall closet, and went out the front door. Will, Bob, and Miller were tossing a football back and forth in the street in front of Will's house. They always had a good time together, even though Bob and Miller were in ninth grade and Will was only in seventh.

"Here, Katie, catch!" Will faked a throw in her direction, his blue eyes teasing as always.

"Can't," she called. "Have to go to my job."

"Hey. What job?" Bob asked, expertly catching the toss from Will.

"I'm doing some baby-sitting," Katie said proudly, "down at the Stellans'."

"Oh, man!" Bob grinned and aimed the ball at Miller. "Look who's growing up!"

"We'll come and help you tonight, Katie," Will said.

"Oh, I won't need any help." Katie laughed. She wouldn't mind if Will came, but that probably wouldn't go over too well with Mrs. Stellan. Anyway, he was just kidding. She hiked her bag up on her shoulder and started off down the street. She had to hurry now. She had a job to do!

After she rang the Stellans' doorbell, Katie experienced real panic. She and Annie — all by themselves. What if Annie wouldn't go to bed . . . or to sleep? What if someone did come to the door? "You're not to open it," Mom had said. And there were those funny noises you could hear at night when a house was quiet.

"Katie! How nice, you're here." Mrs. Stellan was opening the door and welcoming her in. "Wallace, Annie," she called toward the back of the house. "Katie's here." Mrs. Stellan looked great, in a dark red dress and black heels.

In a minute Mr. Stellan, followed by Annie, came into the living room. He had dark hair and dark, thick eyebrows. Annie stood behind him, clutching his leg and peering out at Katie. "How are you, Katie? Nice you could come and sit for us." He gave Katie a big smile and shook hands with her. Katie liked his shaking hands with her. It made her feel grown-up. And now Annie was smiling up at her, too.

"Hi, Annie," Katie said.

But then Annie said, "Where's Jamie?"

Jamie! Katie heard that with a sinking feeling. She wasn't going to have to get Jamie down here, was she? There was no way she could make him come again; no way she wanted to, either. "Well, uh, he's pretty busy right now, Annie."

"Yes, I tried to tell her that," Mrs. Stellan explained with an understanding smile.

Katie suddenly wondered if she had gotten the job because Annie liked Jamie.

"We were so glad you'd had so much experience taking care of your brother all these years," Mrs. Stellan said.

Katie smiled back, relieved and pleased.

"It's been some experience all right," she admitted.

"I can believe it," Mr. Stellan said with a laugh. "I remember some of the things my brothers and I used to do when we were kids."

Mrs. Stellan shot him a quick glance. "Careful, Wallace," she said softly, glancing down at Annie, who was rolling on the floor with Scratch.

Katie silently agreed. She was sure she could take care of Annie, but why give her any ideas.

"Let me show you around, Katie, and here, let me take your jacket." Mrs. Stellan led Katie through the living room, where there was a long glass-topped coffee table and a big green plant in one corner. Katie wished their living room looked like this. But Jamie would probably wreck a glass table, and Mom didn't have time to be taking care of plants.

"Now, about Annie's supper," Mrs. Stellan was saying as they headed into the kitchen. Mrs. Stellan opened the refrigerator. "You might offer her this cottage cheese and vegetables."

Katie had a fleeting moment of worry. Jamie hated cottage cheese and threw it around the kitchen whenever he got the chance. "Or there's frozen pizza," Mrs. Stellan went on. "You could just heat that in the toaster oven. And here's a can of dog food for Scratch. His dish is outside the back door. After you're through feeding him you can leave him out there. Scratch is a good little watch dog. He'll let you know if anyone's coming."

Then Mrs. Stellan showed her Annie's room. The low bed had a pink and white quilt and a pile of stuffed animals against the headboard. There shouldn't be any problems there, Katie told herself, unless Annie didn't want to get *in* the bed. Mrs. Stellan didn't say anything about a bath, thank heavens. That's what Jamie resisted the most. He hated to get in, yelled like crazy if anyone washed his hair or his ears, and then he hated to get out.

"We have to be going, Marci," Mr. Stellan called from the living room. "We can't keep the boss waiting, you know."

"Okay, I'll hurry," Mrs. Stellan called back to

him. "Katie, come into my bedroom while I finish my makeup."

The bedroom had white curtains and a yellow flowered bedspread. Mrs. Stellan sat down at the dressing table, snapped on the light of her makeup mirror, and began to brush on a little eye shadow. The eye makeup made her brown eyes look even larger and prettier.

"You can let Annie watch TV, Katie," Mrs. Stellan said, "but only the children's programs, nothing else. Then get her to bed by seven, okay?"

Annie ran into the room and leaned up against her mother's knee. "Can Cheri come over?" she asked.

"No, Annie. You already had Cheri over today." Mrs. Stellan smoothed Annie's blond hair. "We're lucky to have a friend so nearby," she said to Katie. "Cheri lives right in back of us."

"Yeah, great," Katie managed to say. She just wished the friend's older sister were more friendly.

Mrs. Stellan glanced around the room. "Would you hand me that jewelry box on the bureau, Katie?"

Katie went over to the bureau and picked up a large red velvet jewelry case. When Mrs. Stellan opened it, Katie saw that it was filled with antique gold and pearl and garnet jewelry, like the kind Mrs. Stellan had been wearing the day they first met. It was the prettiest jewelry Katie had ever seen and she watched with interest as Mrs. Stellan quickly picked out a thin gold and red jeweled bracelet and matching ring, and slipped them on. Katie wished there was time to look at the rest of the jewelry.

Mrs. Stellan gave her short brown hair a quick brush and then got up from the dressing table.

"You look really nice," Katie said.

"Thanks, Katie." Mrs. Stellan smiled. "This is an important night for us. My husband's boss and his wife are having us over for a party. I've left their number by the phone in the den, if you need us. Annie is really a good little girl — most of the time, anyway."

Katie nodded and tried to think of all the things she'd heard her friends say about little sisters.

"We'd better go," Mr. Stellan called again from the living room.

"Coming." Mrs. Stellan hurried them out of the bedroom and back to the living room.

"Katie, would you mind bringing in the newspaper?" Mr. Stellan asked. "It's due soon and we don't like it left out front. It looks as if we're not home."

"Sure, I'd be glad to."

"Hon, where's your coat?" Mr. Stellan asked.

Mrs. Stellan glanced around the living room. "Oh, I thought I brought it out here." She dashed back into her bedroom and returned in a minute wearing a plum-colored wool jacket that matched her dress and her jewelry.

Everything was going fine until the Stellans, followed by Scratch, went toward the back door. Then Annie screwed up her face. "Don't want you to go. Stay . . . stay here. . . ." Her voice rose loudly and tears filled her eyes.

Quick, think of something, Katie told herself. "But, Annie, we're going to have fun. We're going to play some great games. I'll show you the ones I play with Jamie. Come on, let's go get your toys." Katie took Annie by the hand, and to her great relief the little girl stopped crying. "I saw some really neat animals on your bed." She waved to the Stellans as she led Annie toward the hall.

"Bye," Mrs. Stellan called softly as she and Mr. Stellan went out the door. "Be sure to call me if you have any problems."

"I will," Katie promised. It was really funny the way everyone thought there were going to be problems.

The Red Velvet Box

Katie and Annie played with the stuffed animals in Annie's room for almost an hour before Annie began to ask for Jamie again. "Let's go out front and look for Jamie," she begged.

Mr. Stellan had said to pick up the newspaper when it was delivered, so Katie guessed it would be all right. "Okay, but we have to stay right around here."

Katie buttoned Annie into her coat, and pulled on her own jacket. Then she called to Scratch and the three of them went out the front door. Katie remembered to leave the lock off the door so they could get back in again. The street was deserted, but Annie seemed happy just to run around in giddy circles on the lawn and do somersaults. Katie looked up the street at her house. Knowing she couldn't go home now, even if she wanted to, gave her a funny feeling. It was beginning to get dark and lights were on in most of the houses along Apple Street.

"Here he comes!" Annie shouted suddenly. Katie glanced around quickly. It couldn't be Jamie, could it? A dark-haired kid she recognized from school had just turned the corner on his bike and was coming up Apple Street. It was the paper boy.

This must be just what Will was doing now, Katie thought — whizzing along on his bike, tossing papers at all the houses on his route. She wished suddenly that he had this street.

"Thanks," she called as the boy slung the paper into the driveway. She went to pick it up and almost collided with Scratch, who raced past her down the street.

"Scra-a-atch!" Annie wailed. "Where're you going?"

Scratch was tearing after a white cat. "Scratch, come back here!" Katie shouted as he and the cat scuttled around the corner and disappeared.

"Scratch! Here, Scratch!" Katie and Annie both called, but Scratch didn't come. Katie heard him barking in the distance. She couldn't just let him wander off. What if he got lost, or hurt?

"Come on, Annie. Let's go get Scratch." Katie took Annie's hand and together they hurried down around the corner, where they found the little black dog barking furiously at the white cat. The cat, ignoring him and calmly blinking his green eyes, sat smugly on top of a brick wall.

"Scratch, come here!" But Scratch wasn't about

to leave that irritating cat. Katie had to collar him and drag him back up the street, Annie all the time trying to help.

By the time they were back in the house, it was almost six o'clock. Katie helped Annie off with her coat and then hurried to the kitchen to heat the pizza. She decided not to take a chance with the cottage cheese.

While Annie was sitting at the kitchen table eating, Katie opened the can of dog food, some terrible smelling stuff called "More." She dumped it in the dog dish and set it outside the back door. Scratch followed her eagerly, so she guessed it must seem all right to him.

"Good Scratch," Annie called, beating the table. "Eat all your food."

After supper she and Annie went into the den to watch television. When it got to be seven o'clock Katie said it was time to go to bed.

"I don't want to." Annie scowled. For a moment Katie felt panicky. What if Annie wouldn't go to bed? What if she was still up when her parents came home? Then she thought of Jamie.

"Jamie's getting ready for bed now, too," she told Annie. "He's probably putting on his pj's right this minute."

"He is?" Annie looked up at Katie, her blue eyes interested.

"Yes, absolutely." Katie kept telling Annie about Jamie, how he'd be washing his face now and brushing his teeth. Boy, would he ever be furious if he could hear her. But it worked. Pretty soon Katie had Annie tucked under her pink and white quilt with all the stuffed animals around her, except for one that she insisted belonged to Cheri. Then Katie sat on a low chair and read to her until she fell asleep.

Katie decided baby-sitting wasn't that hard. She turned on the night light and shut the door. How quiet the house was suddenly. At home it was never this quiet. The Stellans' house lay around her with its strange, unfamiliar sounds. When the phone rang she jumped and dashed across the hall into the den.

It was Mom. Katie was secretly glad to hear her voice. "Is everything okay, Katie?"

"Of course. It's no big deal, Mom. I just read Annie to sleep."

"Good for you, dear. I knew you could handle it. I called to tell you that Mrs. Darby just phoned. She wants you to baby-sit for them next Saturday night. Their daughter has a date and they need a sitter for that night."

"Oh, wonderful!" Katie beamed into the phone. Her Christmas money was growing already. "That's two jobs, Mom. I can, can't I?"

"Of course," Mom agreed. "But now, about

tonight. You will keep the doors locked, won't you? Do me a favor and check them."

"Okay, Mom." Katie remembered she had locked the front door when they came in and the back door when she fed Scratch. But after she hung up she went around and checked the locks again. Then she went to Annie's door and peeked in. Annie lay like a little lump under the covers in her bed.

Katie closed the door softly and headed back for the den. It was so quiet here. Maybe it would be okay to call Sarah Lou. She was dying to tell her about the second baby-sitting job with the Darbys. Would that be a bad thing, one baby-sitter calling another?

Katie was just eyeing the phone on the table in the den when Scratch began to bark outside. Katie hurried to the kitchen door to let him in before he woke up Annie. She turned on the outside light, but didn't see anyone out there.

"What were you barking at, Scratch?" She crouched down and patted him, then remembered to lock the door. He was probably just lonesome and wanted to come inside, she told herself.

Back in the den, Katie turned on the television, keeping it low. She picked up a magazine from the pile on the table and settled on the couch. Scratch had followed her into the den and stretched out on the floor nearby. She began to thumb through the magazine, looking at the ads for gift ideas.

Maybe she could get Mom some pearl earrings — not real pearls, of course.

Suddenly Scratch began to growl in a low, threatening way. He stood up, his round dark eyes staring toward the window.

"What's the matter, Scratch? Is that cat around again?" Katie went to the den window, which faced the street, and looked out. There was nothing to see up and down Apple Street, just a row of yellow streetlights in the darkness. And up there was her house, all lighted up. Mom would be doing the dishes now, while Dad would be reading to Jamie.

Scratch growled again. "It's okay, Scratch." Katie reached down and patted him. "Good dog. What do you hear?" Katie turned the television off and listened, too. She didn't hear anything and she wished Scratch would stop growling. "It's okay, doggie," she assured him. But when he headed out to the kitchen Katie followed him. He went over to the back door and started leaping up and scratching the door with his paws. No wonder he was named Scratch. "What's the matter, Scratch? Do you want to go back out in the yard?" Katie tried not to feel worried.

She snapped on the outside light and peered through the glass in the door at the dimly lighted yard. Suddenly she heard voices and laughter. Then she saw someone jump behind a bush — someone who looked a lot like Will Madison. When

34

the bush began to shake back and forth and voices began chanting, "Who-o-o-o, who-o-o-o," Katie began to relax.

It was the guys in the neighborhood trying to scare her! So Will had come after all! She wished she could invite them in, but they should leave. She opened the back door. "Go, Scratch, go."

Scratch dashed outside, barked fiercely, then turned and scurried back indoors, satisfied that he'd done his job to protect the house.

"Who-o-o-o," went the voices again.

She had to get rid of them. "I know who you are," Katie called out. "You can't scare me. Go on home, you guys."

"Who-o-o-o . . . us?" they shouted. There was a lot of laughing.

Katie opened the door farther and stepped out on the back porch. "Go get 'em, Scratch!" she teased. She wished he had a more threatening name . . . something like King or Tiger.

Scratch dashed outside again. "Get 'em," she shouted. "Catch those guys." She laughed. "Go on home, you guys. You'll wake up Annie."

"Okay, okay, we're going, Katie." It was Will's voice.

Then another voice came out of the darkness. It was a girl's voice. "Why don't you come on over here?" the voice asked. Katie peered through the dark yard. She saw there was a white gate at the back of the yard. It must open onto Michelle's property and that would be Michelle out there. She must have heard the noise.

"Come on over, you guys," Michelle called again. "I'm making popcorn."

"Sure, sure, why not?" Katie heard the guys saying. She could hear them shuffling through the leaves and she recognized the three familiar figures as they disappeared through the gate.

"See ya later, Katie," they called.

"Good-bye," she answered. "Come here, Scratch." She reached down and pulled the dog back into the house, snapped out the light, and locked the door. Those guys! Coming down here and trying to scare her. It had been fun, but now they'd gone over to Michelle's. It seemed lonelier now with no voices or sounds of any kind.

Katie tiptoed down the hall to Annie's door and peeked into the room. All was quiet, the room shadowed in the dim night light.

As she started back toward the den she noticed that Mrs. Stellan's dressing table light was still on. She had used it when she put on her eye makeup. It should be turned off. It was just wasting electricity. Katie went into the bedroom, past the yellow print bedspread toward the dressing table. A picture of Mr. Stellan sat next to the makeup mirror. On the other side of the mirror was the large red velvet jewelry case, just where Mrs. Stellan had left it.

As Katie reached over to turn off the light, she saw that the jewelry case was empty. She stared at the velvet-lined box. "Where . . . where is it?" She felt dazed. Hadn't she seen the case full of jewelry? Was she dreaming? Katie frowned so hard that it made her head ache.

She knew she had seen a lot of jewelry in that case earlier. But now it was totally empty!

Empty!

Katie stood staring at the empty jewelry box. Had Mrs. Stellan put her jewelry somewhere else? Katie tried to think calmly. She'd been right there while Mrs. Stellan put on her jewelry. Then they all left the room together. Wait a minute. Mrs. Stellan did come back to get her jacket. So maybe she hid it then. But why take it out of the box?

Katie glanced around the room. She noticed the window next to the dressing table. It was unlocked and on the driveway side of the house where it would be easy for someone to climb in and take the jewelry. Oh, but that was crazy! Mrs. Stellan must have put her jewelry somewhere. Of course, she wouldn't go off and leave valuable stuff like that just out on her dressing table. She'd hidden it, just the way Mom always hid her good silver teaspoons at home. Katie glanced around the room again. The jewelry must be here somewhere.

Still, this was pretty weird. Maybe she ought

38

to call Mom, ask her advice. Katie hurried down the hall and into the den. She dialed home quickly. But the line was busy. Who was on the phone there? Well, she'd call Sarah Lou then. Sarah Lou had done so much sitting; she'd know what to do.

She looked up the number of the Tuttles', where Sarah Lou was sitting tonight. As she dialed she saw the phone number Mrs. Stellan had written on a piece of paper. Should she call them? But wouldn't the Stellans think she was pretty nosy, poking around in their bedroom? It would be so hard to explain over the phone.

"Hello?" Good, Sarah Lou answered.

"Sarah Lou?" Katie said. "Can you talk for a minute? I want to ask you something." There'd been other things she'd wanted to talk to Sarah Lou about this evening, like her new baby-sitting job, and the guys all going over to Michelle's. But all that faded from her mind now.

"Sarah Lou, I just wondered if . . . if you'd have any ideas. The weirdest thing has happened."

"What, Katie? What's happened?"

"Well, I just went into Mrs. Stellan's bedroom to turn off the light and. . . ." Katie told her friend about finding the empty jewelry case.

"Oh, I wouldn't worry. She must have hidden it, Katie." Sarah Lou's voice sounded so sure, so experienced. "They all hide their stuff. Mrs. Tuttle does and so does Mrs. Stein. Mrs. Tuttle puts her silver down in the basement, I know, and Mrs. Stein always hides her diamond earrings."

Katie drew in a big breath and began to relax. She sank back in the chair. "I was really getting worried for a minute. And it's so quiet here."

"Katie, I better hang up now. Mrs. Tuttle likes to be able to call me to check on things, so I better not stay on the phone. Don't worry, okay?"

Katie hung up. She felt much better. Of course Mrs. Stellan had hidden the jewelry.

Feeling relieved, Katie walked out to the kitchen for a drink of water. The water splattering in the sink was such a nice, familiar sound.

But after she turned the water off, the house grew quiet again. Was that a creak in the living room just now? She stood in the middle of the kitchen, listening. She made herself tiptoe into the hall. Was that another creak? No, she must be imagining. She went to Annie's door and eased it open.

In the dim light the room looked full of shadows. Annie lay peacefully sleeping. Katie waited to see if any of the shadows would move. But everything was quiet. So quiet! Maybe she would call Mom anyway, and tell her about the jewelry.

Katie had just reached the den when she heard the swish of a car coming up the drive. The Stellans were back. She put the magazine on the coffee table and straightened the couch cushions. Then she hurried to the kitchen to meet the Stellans.

"Mrs. Stellan!" Katie rushed toward her as she came in the door. "I'm so glad you're back!"

"Katie! What is it? Has something happened? Is Annie all right?" A worried look crossed Mrs. Stellan's face.

"Fine. I just looked in at her. She's sound asleep. But Mrs. Stellan, I was wondering if I should call you. You see, I noticed the light was still on in your bedroom."

Mr. Stellan was crowding in the back door behind his wife. "What's going on?" he asked, his dark eyebrows frowning.

"Well, you see, I was just telling Mrs. Stellan. I saw the jewelry case was empty and I — "

"Empty?" Mrs. Stellan interrupted. She looked surprised. "You mean my red velvet case?"

"Yes. There's nothing in it now. I figured you probably hid the jewelry somewhere."

"You better check, Marci," Mr. Stellan said, stepping farther into the kitchen. "She's probably talking about something else."

But Katie knew she wasn't.

"Yes, I will, right away." Mrs. Stellan started down the hall, stopping just long enough to take a quick look into Annie's room. Mr. Stellan and Katie followed. When Mrs. Stellan reached her bedroom door she let out a gasp and ran toward her dressing table.

"Wallace!" she said in a stricken voice. "It's empty!" She stared at the case, then up at her husband and at Katie with a dumbfounded look on her face.

"Katie, you were right! It's gone!"

Mr. Stellan rushed forward to look in the case. "Are you sure it was in here when we left?"

"Yes, yes." Sudden tears shimmered in Mrs. Stellan's brown eyes. "I wore . . . this bracelet and my ring. But I left the rest right here."

"Oh, Mrs. Stellan! I'm so sorry!" Katie felt tears stinging her eyes, too. So it really was gone. The worst had happened. Her voice trembled. "I noticed what pretty jewelry it was and I thought it was there when we left the room. But then I hoped you went back and hid it."

"Oh, no, I didn't. I wish I had. It was so pretty." Mrs. Stellan put her hands up and pressed her cheeks. "It was my grandmother's. She gave it to me. And I loved it so much. I shouldn't have left it like that, but I didn't have time and . . . and. . . . Who could have taken it?"

"There, Hon." Mr. Stellan put his arm around her. "It must be around here somewhere." Mr. Stellan was frowning though. "Maybe Annie took it to play with."

Katie shook her head. "I was with Annie every minute. She never came in here, not even for a second. We played in her room and then we went outside for a little bit. After that I gave her supper. We watched TV and then I put her to bed. I was with her all the time." Katie was feeling more scared by the moment. She couldn't bear to give up the hope that Mrs. Stellan had hidden her jewelry. "When my mom goes out, she . . . uh . . . hides her good silver teaspoons."

"I know, I know. That's what I should have done." Mrs. Stellan's eyes were full of tears. "Who could have done it?" A look of fear suddenly crossed her face. "And, Katie." She rushed over to Katie and put her arms around her. "You were right here — and Annie! You both might have been hurt."

"I'm okay," Katie said. She remembered the creaks in the living room and didn't feel so ashamed that she'd been afraid.

"But Wallace." Mrs. Stellan turned back suddenly to her husband. "Maybe there's still someone around here."

Mr. Stellan frowned. "I doubt it. A thief would want to get away fast." He glanced back at the window by the dressing table. "It'd be a cinch for someone to climb in that window there. I'd better call the police."

"The police?" Katie couldn't help exclaiming.

Mr. Stellan went over to the bedside phone and began to dial.

"I'll just go check Annie's room while you're

doing that," Mrs. Stellan said. "I know Katie says Annie wasn't in here. And she knows she's never to touch my good jewelry, but still. . . ."

Katie followed Mrs. Stellan down the hall to Annie's room. They looked all around while Annie went right on sleeping. Mrs. Stellan even woke her up and asked her if she had seen the jewelry.

"No, Mommie, no," she said sleepily and went back to sleep after getting a comforting hug from her mother.

Katie was feeling more terrible than ever. How could this happen when she was right here? It didn't make sense. The Stellans didn't act as if they thought she'd anything to do with it. Still, they must wonder . . . after all, she was here the whole time.

In a few minutes the front doorbell rang and Mr. Stellan let in two policemen. Katie felt cold, shivery. The police were big and stern looking in their dark uniforms. After the Stellans told them briefly what had happened, they checked all over the house, even the closets, before they went outside.

After a few minutes they came back into the living room. "There's no one around now," they reported. "Let's have the whole story," the tall policeman said. He turned to Katie. "You've been here all evening?"

"Yes, I have. Right here. Or out front for just

a little while. We had to get Scratch, the dog. He ran down around the corner. But I was in here the rest of the time. I know it sounds crazy, but that's what happened. I found the case empty when I went in to turn off the light. I'd seen jewelry in it before Mrs. Stellan left. You see, I was watching her — "

"Watching her?" he asked. His jaw jutted out in a way that seemed very unfriendly.

"Well, yes." Katie explained how they'd been talking while Mrs. Stellan touched up her makeup and put on her jewelry.

The other policeman wrote everything down. Then he asked for Katie's name and address; what time she had arrived; what time the Stellans went out; and if Katie had been there baby-sitting other times.

"No, this is my first night," Katie said.

"You're new?" the tall policeman asked sharply. "Anything else happen here this evening?"

Katie hesitated. "Some kids in the neighborhood came around. They knew I was going to be here," she explained.

"Who were they?" Katie didn't want to give the names, but she knew she had to. After she'd told them, she added, "They weren't trying to make trouble. It was just a joke. They would never come in the house and take anything."

"Were there any other juveniles around?" She hated the way he said juveniles.

"Uh, well, there was Michelle. She was by her back fence." Katie looked at the Stellans. "She must've heard them." The policeman made her explain who Michelle was and where she lived.

All this time the Stellans sat silently, listening. What were they thinking? Were they angry because her friends had been down here? But she'd tried to get rid of them. And besides, they didn't take the jewelry.

Mrs. Stellan described the jewelry to the police. "It was a matching set, you see, of garnets and pearls. It was my grandmother's. She would feel so bad if she knew I'd lost it. It's been in our family for such a long time." Mrs. Stellan was almost begging the policemen to find it for her.

"Hey, Hon." Mr. Stellan put his arm around his wife. "Take it easy. We'll find whoever it was." Mr. Stellan was frowning fiercely with those dark eyebrows of his. "Could you get any fingerprints?" he asked the policemen.

The policemen shook their heads. "We tried," the tall one answered. "Can't get a thing off that velvet, you know."

The police stood up, ready to leave. As they went toward the door, Katie was startled to hear the tall one say, "It doesn't look like the work of a pro, ma'am. It looks more like kids, I'd guess.

Maybe someone in the neighborhood. We'll check."

Katie drew in a quick breath, shocked at what he was saying. And then, as he went out the front door, she heard him add, in a low voice, something about "a new sitter here tonight."

Katie felt sick. He meant her!

Will Offers
To Help

Katie had a terrible time going to sleep that night. She couldn't stop thinking of her talk with the Stellans, the police, and then her own parents. Everyone was so upset and worried. It had been frightening. The jewelry really was gone, and she wondered what the Stellans would think of her now. Would they ever hire her again? She couldn't forget what the policeman had said about a new sitter.

In the morning, before breakfast, Katie called Sarah Lou and told her what had happened.

"Katie, that's terrible. You poor kid." Sarah Lou's voice was warm and sympathetic.

"It's rotten, all right." Katie squeezed her eyes shut for a minute to keep back the sudden tears.

"I was just a little worried when you called me last night," Sarah Lou confessed. "But I couldn't believe — " Sarah Lou broke off.

"I know. I couldn't, either, Sarah Lou. Even now, this morning, it still seems impossible."

Later, as Katie sat with her family at the table in the dining room, the sunshine streaming through the windows onto the green, leafy wallpaper, last night seemed like a bad dream.

"It's just weird," she said for about the tenth time. "I don't understand how anyone could come in and steal the jewelry when I was right there."

"It is strange," her mother agreed. "The thought of you being there with some criminal around really scares me." She passed Katie a plate of whole wheat toast. "Eat something, dear," she urged. But Katie didn't feel hungry.

"I wonder if the Stellans will ever ask me to baby-sit again. I just hope they don't think I had anything to do with it." Katie frowned and her stomach went sort of tight.

"They'd better not." Her dad straightened his glasses on his nose, frowning a little. "Or I'll fix 'em just like that." He picked up an empty yogurt carton and crushed it into a ball, grinning suddenly at Katie.

"Thanks, Dad." She was able to smile a little.

"Yeah, but it sounds as if the police suspect some kids in the neighborhood," Dick put in, piling scrambled eggs onto his plate.

"Well, they better not blame any of us," Jamie said. He stabbed at a piece of scrambled egg. Katie was comforted by this show of loyalty, but the problem remained.

"Mrs. Stellan was really upset about losing her jewelry."

"I can sympathize with her, Katie," Mom said. "I know I'd be sad if I lost my grandmother's teaspoons." The last time Mom hid the twelve heirloom spoons the whole family had to help hunt for them. They finally turned up in a drawer of Dad's old socks.

"Another thing," Mom went on, "I'm a little worried about you going out baby-sitting now. You're supposed to go to the Darbys' Saturday night." She frowned as she sipped a glass of milk.

"Please don't worry, Mom," Katie said. Actually Katie felt a little uneasy herself about going to the Darbys', but she didn't want to admit it. The thought of being alone again in someone's house with some thief outside was just a little bit creepy.

"But it isn't going to happen to Katie again," Dad said. "Not likely, anyway." He gave Katie a reassuring smile.

After breakfast Katie decided to go down to the Stellans' to see if there was any news about the jewelry. When she stepped out the front door she saw a police car parked in front of Will's house, and a policeman was just leaving. Was he there because of last night? When the car drove off, Katie ran across the front yard. She must tell Will it was her fault, that she'd had to tell the police who was there. Katie ran up the front steps of

Will's house and rang the bell. In a minute he opened the door.

"Will!" She burst out. "Why was that policeman here? Did it have anything to do with the Stellans?"

To her relief Will didn't appear angry. "They think I'm a jewel thief, that's all." He stuck his hands in the hip pockets of his jeans and lounged against the front door. He didn't seem a bit worried and already Katie felt better. Will, with his teasing blue eyes and freckled nose, looked as cheerful as usual.

"I'm sorry. They asked me who was around last night. You've heard all about it, I guess."

"Yeah, they told me. They're going around checking everybody's story. They went to Bob's and to Miller's earlier this morning and now they'll probably go to Michelle's."

Katie groaned. "Oh no! I hope she won't be mad. I hope everybody doesn't think I'm just a big rat!"

Will grinned at her. "You don't look like one."

Katie felt a moment's pleasure. Will wasn't mad at her. In fact, right at this moment he looked as if he liked her.

"I was just going to the Stellans' to see if they've found out anything."

"Yeah?" Will's blue eyes looked interested. "Why don't I go with you?"

Katie felt pleased. "Sure, come on."

They hurried down Apple Street together. But when they knocked on the Stellans' front door and rang the bell, there was no answer.

"I'd say they're not here." Will shrugged.

Katie frowned. She didn't hear Scratch barking, so he must be gone, too. She went down the steps and began to circle the front of the house. "It's really weird the way that jewelry disappeared," she said. "I can't believe I wouldn't have heard someone climb in the window in the bedroom."

They both walked around to the driveway and looked at the bedroom window. "It'd be easy enough to climb in there," Will said. "But there's no sign of any clues, like, you know, footprints or anything." Will examined the ground beneath the window.

"Let's check under the other windows," Katie suggested. They headed toward the front of the house again, looking around the bushes and in the dirt beneath all the windows.

Suddenly Katie leaned forward. "Will! Look!" There was part of a footprint. She bent down and brushed away a couple of leaves. In the soft dirt next to the bushes was a big, clear footprint.

Will let out a long, low whistle.

Katie stood up. "Someone must have been standing here. Oh, wow! Will, this is by the den window." She frowned, remembering last night. "That's where Annie and I were sitting, watching TV."

"Hey-y-y, Katie." Will glanced at her, sympathy in his blue eyes; then he, too, bent over to examine the ground. "It looks like a guy's footprint all right." He put his foot next to it; the print was larger. "And see, it's got a U-shaped mark on the sole." Will lifted his foot to inspect the bottom of his sneakers. "Not guilty." He grinned.

"I know that," Katie laughed. "Maybe we ought to cover this up in case it rains, just till I can show it to the Stellans." They placed some leaves carefully over the print and checked the dirt under the rest of the windows. They even went through the driveway gate into the backyard, but there were no other footprints close to the house. They peered over the fence into Michelle's yard, but saw nothing unusual. Staring at the back of Michelle's house reminded Katie of the police. What would Michelle think of being questioned by the police? It wouldn't be good, Katie felt sure.

"You know, the police said it looked like kids — in the neighborhood," Katie confided to Will as they walked home. "It couldn't be anyone we know, could it?" She frowned, glancing up the quiet street. It seemed totally impossible.

"No, no way," Will scoffed.

"But maybe Bob or Miller made that footprint when they were down here last night."

Will kicked at some leaves on the sidewalk. "I don't think so," he said thoughtfully. "We all came down Apple together. We were laughing and talking about how we were going to fool you. But all we did was walk down the driveway and go in the backyard. Then after that we went over to Michelle's for a while."

"I know." Katie wanted to ask if they'd had a great time and how long they'd stayed, but she didn't.

"When we left we went home by Michelle's street. We never came over to the Stellans' again. Of course, you could ask Miller and Bob. Maybe they did something later I don't know about."

"Maybe it's an old footprint. Maybe it didn't even happen last night."

"Yeah, could've been Mr. Stellan," Will agreed.

"Or the police," Katie suggested. "They were looking around outside last night. But they seemed more interested in the bedroom window on the side of the house, not the den window in front. I just hope the Stellans don't think I had anything to do with it." It hurt to say that, even to Will.

"Katie, they'd be crazy to think that. Besides, maybe this footprint will prove you're innocent. See? You've got a clue. Katie, the detective," Will said, his blue eyes teasing her.

"So who could I follow around after? You know in books detectives are always shadowing suspects."

"You can shadow me," Will said.

Katie groaned. Will could never be serious for

very long. They were in front of his house now and he looked straight at her, and added, "I'll help when you get ready to go after somebody."

"Thanks, Will. Thanks a lot." She smiled gratefully at him and started toward her house. But who in the world would they go after, anyway?

Unfriendly
Michelle

The next morning Katie was relieved to see a dry street and blue sky. Good! At least it hadn't rained during the night so the footprint should still be there. Her mom and dad said the police had already checked out the yard and to let them take care of it. But Katie wanted to follow up on the clue herself.

She'd called the Stellans yesterday but there hadn't been any answer. She'd go down after school, but first she'd talk to Bob and Miller about the footprint. If they had made it, either of them, then she wouldn't want to go telling on them.

As soon as they were all settled in Dick's car and starting off for school, Katie burst out with her question. "When you guys came down to the Stellans' Saturday night, did you happen to come up close to any of the windows?" She was in the backseat between Jamie and Will, as usual. Bob and Miller sat up front with Dick, their shoulders big in their bulky jackets.

"Hey, Katie!" Bob turned around, surprise on his broad face. "You mean, look in the window? Katie, we wouldn't do that — go staring in people's windows. We might've really scared you. We didn't go near the house, did we, Miller?"

"No way, Katie." Miller gave her a quick look. "Why'd you think that? Did you see someone hanging around out there?"

"No, I just saw a footprint with a U-shaped mark on it."

"Katie, the detective!" Miller grinned at her. Then he looked at Bob. "Come on, Bob, let's see the bottom of your shoe." The two of them started laughing and grabbing and checking each other's shoes. "Of course I might have changed my shoes, ya know," Miller joked.

"Yeah, and what about Dick's shoes?" Bob said.

"Hey, watch it," Dick protested. "I'm driving."

"Here's my shoe." Jamie kicked his foot in the air.

"Come on, you guys," Katie pleaded.

"Don't laugh," Will told the others, his blue eyes serious. "Katie's going to solve this mystery, with my help."

She felt pleased he had added that.

When Jamie climbed out of the car at his school, he promised Katie he'd check all the kids' shoes. She didn't have the heart to tell him the kids were too small.

As they headed on to Katie and Will's school, Miller looked over his shoulder at Katie with a little smile. "I didn't know you were going to send the police after us, Katie."

"Sorry about that. I couldn't help it. They asked me who was around."

"I told 'em plenty," Miller said in mock seriousness. "They looked at all my shoes, too."

Katie knew Miller wasn't angry with her, but how was Michelle going to feel about *her* visit from the police?

Dick stopped the car in the parking lot of the junior high, and Katie and Will jumped out. Will jogged off to the athletic field. Katie, looking around for her friends, followed a crowd of kids into the school building. She saw Sarah Lou and Jody walking down the hall together and ran to catch up with them. "Hi," she called, "Sarah Lou! Jody!" She had talked to them both on the telephone yesterday.

"Hi, Katie!" They turned with smiling faces and closed around her. It was so good to be with her friends again.

"Any more news?" Sarah Lou asked, her round face eager.

"Just the footprint. Nothing else," Katie said.

"Who do *you* think took the jewelry?" Jody frowned and shook back her short dark hair. "Are you sure you didn't hear anything or see anybody?"

"No," Katie said. "I didn't see anyone, except Will and the other guys in the neighborhood." It helped to share her worries with her friends. "Anyway, whoever made the footprint has a U-shape on the sole of his shoe."

Jody glanced around at the kids streaming through the halls. "Oh, wow! There could be a million people with shoes or sneakers like that. How will you ever find the right one?"

"You'll have to think of something, Katie," Sarah Lou teased. "So you can get Will's help."

Katie got a happy feeling whenever she thought about Will. It was so neat of him to offer to help. "Well, I am planning to do something this afternoon. I'm going to see Mrs. Stellan and show her that footprint."

At lunchtime Katie thought of looking for Michelle and telling her that she was sorry about the police coming to her house. But Michelle seemed to be avoiding her.

Katie decided to do the same. She even tried to convince herself that maybe the police hadn't gone to Michelle's after all.

Between math and social studies Katie went to the office to phone Mrs. Stellan. She wanted to tell her to go outside to look at the footprint. The sky had suddenly grown very dark and if it rained, her only clue could be washed away.

The secretary let her use the phone, but there

was no answer at Mrs. Stellan's. When the bell started ringing for the next class, Katie let out such a groan that the secretary asked her if she needed to see the school nurse.

"Oh, no, I'm okay," Katie said. But she wasn't. She felt half sick. What if the footprint got washed away and the police hadn't seen it?

Katie got home that afternoon before it rained. She tossed her backpack in the house and rushed down the street to Mrs. Stellan's. As she hurried along, a sudden wonderful fantasy gripped her! Mrs. Stellan had found the jewelry somehow, some way.

Katie ran past the Goldbergs' house, next door to the Stellans', and turned up the walk to the small white house. She rang the bell and waited, staring hard at the green front door. In a moment Mrs. Stellan pulled open the door.

"Hello, Katie. You've been running." Mrs. Stellan's brown eyes looked friendly.

Katie gulped to catch her breath. Mrs. Stellan was smiling. Maybe she *had* found her jewelry!

"Mrs. Stellan, did you find out anything — about the jewelry, I mean?"

"No, the police haven't been able to discover a thing." Mrs. Stellan's brown eyes looked sad now.

Katie felt like sagging against the wall of the house, she was so disappointed.

"Won't you come in, Katie?" Mrs. Stellan asked.

"Annie has her little friend here and — "

"Katie!" Annie came crowding to the door behind her mother. "Hi, Katie," Annie cried. "See, Cheri is here." Annie looked terribly pleased as she grabbed her friend.

Behind both of them appeared dark-haired, unsmiling Michelle. Why did she have to be here just now when Katie wanted to show Mrs. Stellan the footprint? What if it was Mr. Stellan's? That could be pretty embarrassing.

Katie turned to Mrs. Stellan. "Yesterday I came down to see you and you weren't home and I . . . uh. . . ." This was going to be hard to explain — why she was poking around down here. "I was trying to figure out how the thief might've gotten into your house."

"Oh, yes?" Mrs. Stellan's brown eyes focused on Katie with interest.

"I found this footprint. Let me show you. I don't know if you've seen it or not."

"No, I don't think so," Mrs. Stellan said.

Katie started down the front steps toward the lawn. Mrs. Stellan and the girls followed her.

"I was afraid it was going to rain. I called you yesterday, but you weren't home."

"We went to Newtown to visit my grandmother," Mrs. Stellan explained. "She's in a nursing home there and it's a long drive. I didn't tell her about the jewelry." Mrs. Stellan's voice broke.

Poor Mrs. Stellan, Katie felt so sorry for her.

They had reached the den window now, and Katie knelt down by the footprint. "There's this one footprint. I thought maybe someone was looking in the den, maybe spying on the place, you know? I covered it up with some leaves to protect it." Katie carefully removed the leaves to reveal the large footprint still in the dirt. "Of course I suppose it could be Mr. Stellan's," she added quickly.

Katie heard Michelle snicker behind her.

"Where? Where?" Annie said.

"Wait, stay back, Annie." Mrs. Stellan bent over for a minute, then straightened up. "Katie, I think that's probably Joe's."

"Joe's? Who's Joe?" She stared at Mrs. Stellan, not understanding.

"I hired the Goldbergs' yardman. He came to work Friday for the first time," Mrs. Stellan explained.

Katie heard Michelle laugh.

"And you see, that's right where he would have to step to turn on the faucet for the hose."

"Ha-ha," Michelle laughed. "The yardman!"

Katie saw all right. Why hadn't she noticed the faucet? "I didn't know you had a yardman." What else could she say? She felt her face burning!

"Why don't you come in the house?" Mrs. Stellan said kindly.

Katie numbly followed her into the house. How

embarrassing! Katie, the big sleuth, the detective, had messed up such a simple clue.

"Did you see the write-up in the paper?" Mrs. Stellan picked up a clipping from the glass-topped table. "It was in the morning edition."

"The paper?" Katie echoed. "You mean about the jewelry?" It was written up in the paper? Katie hadn't thought of that. What did it say about her?

"I already read it," Michelle said. "Everyone has." Her dark eyes looked smug.

"I haven't," Katie said. She took the clipping, but she dreaded reading it. "Thefts in Hemsted over the Weekend. A thief made off with valuable old family jewelry from a house on Apple Street while a young baby-sitter was in the house Saturday evening. . . ." Katie drew in a quick breath. She was the sitter! The sitter who couldn't even hear a thief come in the house. Who maybe knew something about it. Would anyone want to hire a sitter like that? Would Mrs. Stellan again? Or Mrs. Darby? At least the article didn't mention her name. Still, people would be asking and the news would spread.

"It'll probably be in the afternoon paper, too." Michelle seemed to be gloating.

"The publicity could help get my jewelry back." Mrs. Stellan sounded hopeful. "It's not the kind you'd see every day."

"I'll bet!" Michelle said. "What was it like?" Her dark eyes were wide and interested.

"Oh, there was the prettiest coronet, like a headband, with garnets and pearls and diamond chips . . . and earrings that were gold hearts covered with garnets . . . and a string of garnets, and . . . ." Mrs. Stellan broke off with a sigh.

"Bet you could never find any like it today," Michelle said.

Oh, that Michelle, Katie thought. Why didn't she go home and take her bets with her.

"If the thief tries to sell it," Mrs. Stellan said, "someone might recognize it."

"The whole thing's a terrible shame," Michelle said. She shot a sudden glance at Katie, her eyes blazed dark and angry as if she'd been waiting for this moment. "My mom sure didn't like that visit from the police."

"Well, I'm sorry," Katie said. "The police asked who was around that night, and you were around."

Michelle shook back her hair crossly. "Cheri and I have to go now. Good-bye Mrs. Stellan. Bye, Annie."

A Wonderful Surprise

As Michelle and Cheri were leaving by the back door, the phone rang. Mrs. Stellan hurried into the den to answer it and Katie waited with Annie in the living room.

"Watch me, Katie," the little girl begged, trying to hop on one foot.

"That was Wallace," Mrs. Stellan said when she came back into the living room. "He had to go to Chicago on business. He just called to say he got there safely." She looked around the living room as if she missed him already.

Katie knew how much Mom missed Dad when he had to go away. "Want me to stay and play with Annie for a little while?" she asked.

"Katie, that would be wonderful." Mrs. Stellan's brown eyes brightened at the offer. "If you can stay with Annie right now, I could run to the market. Wallace suggested I ask you to help me out while he's gone."

Katie beamed. "I'd be glad to." So she was still

going to be their sitter; even Mr. Stellan had suggested it. That made her feel good, especially after she'd had such a rotten time with Michelle. Of course she'd known Michelle wasn't going to like that visit from the police.

Mrs. Stellan bustled around. In a few minutes she had her purse slung over her shoulder and was ready to leave.

"Good-bye, sweetie. I'll be back soon. You can play with Katie, okay?"

Annie's mouth turned down. "Where are you going?" Her voice sounded teary.

"Just to the market. I'll bring you a surprise, how's that? All right?" She knelt and hugged Annie, then hurried toward the back door. "I'd love it if you could get her out for a little while, Katie. It looks as if it isn't going to rain after all," Mrs. Stellan said as she went out the back door.

"Mommy!" Annie cried after her.

"Come on, Annie. Let's go outside and see Scratch. You know, Jamie thinks Scratch is just the neatest dog. He really likes your dog." Katie kept talking fast while she got Annie into her jacket.

The air felt fresh when they stepped outside and there were patches of blue sky. It was a good yard for a little kid, all enclosed by a high white fence and with a gate across the driveway. How could she entertain Annie? Katie wondered. She looked so unhappy. Poor little kid, she'd miss her dad while he was away, too.

Katie spotted a frisbee on the ground. "Here, Annie, let's play." She felt pretty good now. At least the Stellans seemed to trust her and want her around.

"Catch, Annie!" Katie threw the frisbee.

Annie tried to sail the frisbee back to Katie but it curved over behind the bushes at the back of the yard.

"I'll get it, Annie." As Katie ran toward the bushes she noticed Scratch for the first time. He was at the back of the yard and he seemed to be chewing on something. Katie went over to him, expecting to see an old bone or a toy in his mouth. But when she got close she saw he was holding something shiny between his sharp white teeth!

Katie bent down and tried to ease the glittery object out of his mouth but Scratch wouldn't let go. "Don't bite it, Scratch!" Katie yelled.

But Scratch kept shaking his head, flapping his ears, and growling. He thought she was playing. What did he have anyway? It looked like something made of gold.

"Annie!" Katie called frantically. "Come, play with Scratch. I'm trying to get his mouth open. He's got something in it, something terrific!"

Annie came running over and got down on her hands and knees and began to circle the dog.

"That's good, Annie. Keep it up!"

Finally Scratch barked at Annie, and the gold chain fell out of his mouth onto the ground. Katie darted for it and snatched it up in the air. It was a thick gold bracelet. And a red jeweled heart hung from the clasp.

"Oh, look!" Katie shouted and started dancing around the yard. "Look at this bracelet, Annie . . . this gorgeous bracelet!"

Annie stretched out her arms. "Pretty, pretty. Is that Mommy's?"

"I think it is, Annie! I think it's your mom's. I think we found your mom's bracelet!" Katie threw back her head and laughed. "Isn't that terrific? The thief must've dropped it as he ran through the yard. Maybe there's more here." Katie ran over and put the bracelet on the ledge of the kitchen window. "C'mon, Annie. Let's keep looking. Let's hunt for some more jewelry."

"More jewelry? Okay-y-y," Annie sang out. "I like to find jewelry!" Annie and Scratch started to run around the yard in circles while Katie crawled over the ground on her hands and knees. Suddenly the yard seemed awfully big. There was so much grass, so many bushes, so many places to look. Katie groaned with impatience. Oh, if only she could find more of the jewelry.

"This isn't easy, Annie." She resumed crawling slowly back and forth.

Suddenly she heard the rear gate open and heard Michelle and Cheri come into the yard.

"Hi," Michelle said, looking amused. "What're you doing? Looking for more great clues?"

"Cheri-i-i!" Annie ran toward Michelle's sister.

"Better than that," Katie said triumphantly. "I'm hunting for more of the jewelry. We just found a bracelet." Katie pointed toward the window ledge. Let Michelle laugh at that! "I'm sure it's Mrs. Stellan's bracelet."

"Oh, yeah?" Michelle grinned. "So you decided to come up with some of it?"

Katie was furious. "Look, Michelle, I didn't take the jewelry and I don't know who did. Annie and I happened to find that bracelet in the yard just now. The dog had it."

"The dog?" Michelle burst out laughing, flipping her dark hair. "You're kidding!"

"It's true. You can believe it or not." Katie turned away and started searching the yard again. She wished Michelle would go home. Maybe the story did sound sort of crazy, but it was true.

Michelle stood there smoothing her bangs and watching Katie. "My mom says everyone on our block has seen the story in the newspaper and they all want to know who the sitter was." Michelle gave a crooked little smile.

"And I suppose you told them?" Katie said. She had felt so good about finding the bracelet, now everything Michelle said made her feel terrible.

"Wel-l-l, they want to know. My mom was pretty mad about having the police come and question us, especially since I didn't have anything to do with it. All the neighbors kept asking us what was going on. My mom said it didn't make us look good, since we're new and all."

"I'm sorry, Michelle. I couldn't help it. The police asked who was around."

"It still seems funny you didn't hear the thief the other night."

"I know." Katie paused and frowned. "Finding that bracelet out here makes me think the thief came through the backyards here." She waved her hand in the direction of Michelle's house. "Through your yard and this one, then ran out the same way and dropped the bracelet on the way."

"Look, Katie, leave me and my yard out of this." Michelle's dark eyes stared coldly at Katie. "First you send the police over, now you're trying to cook up some crazy theory about our yard."

She turned abruptly. "Come on, Cheri." The two little girls were just opening the back door.

"I want to play with Annie's toys."

Michelle shook her head. "No, Cheri. Not now. Mom said to go for a walk." She shot a threatening glance toward Katie. "Just watch what you say, Katie Hart. Come on, Cheri, let's go up the street and find someone else to talk to."

After they had gone Katie tried to put Michelle and the story in the newspaper out of her mind. Katie just hoped Mrs. Darby would still want her to come on Saturday.

"Katie, can I go out front?" Annie asked.

"Sure, Annie. Let's just put the bracelet inside." Finding the bracelet like that in the backyard probably did look sort of funny. She hoped Mrs. Stellan would believe her.

When Katie and Annie got out front, there was a further disappointment for Katie.

As she looked up the street she saw Will with his daily stack of newspapers, and Michelle and Cheri were with him. Michelle was folding Will's newspapers, too — bending over, putting them in the bags on Will's bike.

Katie let out a groan and sank down on the front steps. Why couldn't it start raining right now? She propped her chin in her hands and stared moodily up the street.

"What's the matter, Katie?" Annie sat down close to her. "Your stomach hurt?"

"No, Annie." Katie put her arm around the little girl and hugged her. "It's nothing much. Just everything, actually. Come on. Let's go play frisbee again."

They were playing in the backyard when they heard Mrs. Stellan's car in the driveway. Katie dashed into the house to get the bracelet. Mrs.

Stellan was just opening the driveway gate, carrying a bag of groceries, when Katie hurried back outside.

"Mrs. Stellan, look what I found!" Katie held out the bracelet. As the story spilled out, Mrs. Stellan looked first incredulous, then amazed. At last she looked pleased, really pleased. She held her bracelet up in the air and watched it sparkle in the late afternoon sunlight.

Katie began to feel happy again, too. If this piece had been found, somehow the rest of it would turn up also.

The Perfect Suspect

That evening Mrs. Darby called Katie and canceled her baby-sitting date. She said their plans had changed and they didn't need a sitter after all. Katie wondered if it was true or if they just didn't want her. All evening she kept thinking about the Darbys. Even after she got in bed, she kept tossing and turning and worrying. If only there was something she could do. Something Mrs. Stellan had said kept floating around in the back of her mind. It was something about the thief trying to sell the jewelry. That was it! Where would someone try to get rid of the jewelry?

Then the answer flashed right through her brain. At a swap meet! Katie sat straight up in bed. Every weekend when the weather was good there was a swap meet in Bigby's Field. That was just the place where someone might try to unload jewelry. She could go and check it out. Maybe Will would go with her. She snuggled down under the covers, and closed her eyes, able to relax at last. In the morning she'd talk to Will.

But the next morning when Katie climbed into the backseat of Dick's car, Will was not there. Miller and Bob were in the front seat, as usual, with Dick, and only Jamie was in the back.

"Where's Will?" Katie asked.

"He's sick today," Dick said and pulled away from the curb.

Katie tried to hide her disappointment. She wanted so much to talk to him about the swap meet. She hoped he wouldn't think it was a crazy idea.

As they turned onto Elm Street they passed Michelle standing on her corner, waiting for the bus. Katie pretended not to see her, but she knew Michelle was watching them.

At least she wouldn't get to help Will with his papers today, Katie thought. But . . . wait a minute! Who. . . ? Katie leaned forward. "Who'll do Will's paper route this afternoon if he's sick?" she asked.

Dick shrugged. "Maybe his mom."

"I've got a football game," Bob explained. "We're going to beat Elmira, too."

"Yeah," Miller added. "Can't miss that."

So the guys couldn't help Will. "I suppose I could do it," Katie said.

"Can I help you fold them? Can I?" Jamie bounced around on the seat and jabbed Katie with his elbow.

"Ouch! Only if you sit still and stop poking me," Katie said. "Anyway, maybe Will isn't really sick.

Maybe he'll be okay by this afternoon." Katie had planned to go down to the Stellans' after school to see if any more of the jewelry had turned up. Mrs. Stellan had said she was going to search the yard again.

When Katie got to school she hurried off to find her friends.

"Sarah Lou, Jody," she called when she saw them walking toward the athletic field.

"Hi, Katie." They turned to wait for her. "Any more jewelry turn up since you called me?" Sarah Lou asked, eagerly.

"Not that I know of." Katie decided not to mention her plan to go to the swap meet until she talked to Will. It could be a crazy idea.

"Sarah Lou told me Michelle gave you a bad time about finding the bracelet."

"Yeah, really bad." Katie nodded her head.

"She's mean! *She's* probably the one who took it." Sarah Lou tossed her ponytail.

"She was helping Will with his papers again yesterday," Katie added.

Jody rolled her eyes. "How did Will like that?"

"I don't know. He's sick today."

"After being with Michelle, no wonder!" Sarah Lou grinned.

Just then Katie looked past Sarah Lou and saw Michelle heading toward them. "Sh-h-h, Michelle's coming," she warned.

They all stopped laughing and moved closer together as Michelle came up to them. "Hi," she said. "I saw you driving by this morning."

Katie tried not to feel guilty. They could have offered her a ride in the car, she realized.

"Do you get to go in the car with all those boys every day?"

"Well, yes. Two of them are my brothers."

Michelle didn't say anything for a minute. Then she added, "I didn't see Will Madison in the car."

"He's sick today." That Michelle! She noticed everything.

Michelle raised her eyebrows. She did have nice, dark eyes. "Hm-m-m. Who'll do his paper route?" she asked.

"Oh, his mom," Katie said quickly. "I . . . uh . . . I might help her."

Michelle grinned slightly. "Well, if you need any more help. . . ."

"I don't think she will," Sarah Lou said with a toss of her blond ponytail.

"Maybe I'll call him up and ask how he's doing. See ya." Michelle strolled off.

Katie stood looking after her. She shouldn't let this bother her so . . . just because Michelle wanted to be friendly with everyone else in the neighborhood.

"Do you think she likes Will?" Jody asked.

"Doesn't she know Will likes you?" Sarah Lou said.

"Well, listen now," Katie protested, "I don't know that." She wished she did. "Besides, even if he does, he could change his mind and start liking someone else."

"Well, not her, I hope," Sarah Lou said.

Katie decided that she would definitely offer to help with the paper route. It would be a nice thing to do. After all, Will had said he would help her. Maybe she'd do the whole thing on her bike. Why not?

When she rang the Madisons' doorbell that afternoon, Will's mother answered.

"Hello, Katie," Mrs. Madison said. "Will's upstairs in bed, I'm afraid." Mrs. Madison was dressed in her jogging suit with a headband on her short, gray hair. She and Mom often went jogging around the block together.

"I'm sorry Will's sick," Katie said, lingering in the doorway. "Do you suppose I could talk to him?"

"Who's that?" Will's voice came from the head of the stairs.

"It's Katie," his mother called over her shoulder to him. "I don't think you'd better come down." She motioned to Katie to step inside. "He's got a terrible stomach bug. Better not get too close to him."

Katie went toward the stairs. "Hi, Will."

"Hi, Katie." Will leaned over the railing. He was wearing a blue bathrobe that made his eyes look even bluer.

"Sorry you're sick."

"Yeah, I barfed five times today."

Katie stepped back. "Don't tell me about it," she laughed.

"Yes, Will, please!" his mother protested.

"I've come to see if I could do you a favor," Katie said.

"Yeah?" Will grinned down at her. "I know. You brought me my homework? Or some brownies?" He clutched his stomach again and groaned. "Uh-h-h, just what I need."

"Come on!" Katie protested. "It's better than that. I'll do your paper route for you, if you want."

"Hey." Will looked down at her with surprise. "That'd be okay, wouldn't it, Mom?"

"It sure would." Mrs. Madison looked pleased. "I wasn't looking forward to delivering those papers. I could help you get them ready, Katie."

"Thanks, but Jamie can help me fold them," Katie said.

"I'll go get Will's route list for you. It's out in the kitchen." Mrs. Madison hurried off toward the kitchen.

"Thanks, Katie, for helping. You're all heart." He grinned at her.

Katie felt like saying something about how he'd

had another helper the other day, but she didn't want to act as if she was spying on him. Besides, she wanted to ask him what he thought about going to the swap meet.

"Why don't you use my bike, too?" Will suggested.

"Okay, that might be easier. But listen, Will, I wanted to ask you something. What do you think about going to the swap meet on Saturday?" She told him her plan.

"Great idea," Will agreed when she'd finished. "Swap meets are fun, too. Maybe we'll even find the jewelry."

Katie liked the way Will had said we, and she kept thinking about Saturday as she pedaled along, delivering papers that afternoon. It would be exciting to go somewhere with Will. It was like having a date, almost, she thought with a little shiver of pleasure. She couldn't wait to tell Sarah Lou.

It was getting late as she tossed the newspapers on the driveways along Railroad and Prospect streets. She was just finishing the route when she saw another kid on a bike with canvas news-paper sacks. As they pedaled toward each other she recognized Mike, the dark-haired boy who delivered on Apple Street. Will had told her his name. He had been so disappointed when

Mike signed up first and got Apple Street.

"Hi," Katie called out as they passed each other. Then as she biked home something about Mike kept going around in her mind. Finally it hit her, hit her so hard she almost fell off Will's bike. Mike was on Apple Street the night of the theft. He was there just when she and Annie were busy chasing Scratch around the corner. They weren't gone very long, but time enough for him to run into the house and out again and — Katie glanced down at the canvas newspaper bags. These bags would be a good place to hide the jewelry.

"Wait!" she called, looking back. But Mike had already turned the corner and was nowhere in sight. If only she could ask him some questions. It was rotten to be suspecting someone she knew, a kid from school. But still, someone did it. Why hadn't she thought of Mike before?

As Katie was heading for home, she kept building a case against Mike. Maybe it was Mike and not Joe who had made the footprint. He might have looked in the den window first, before he ran into the house. Maybe she and Will together could ask him some questions, things like, "Where were you the night of. . . ?" No, cleverer than that. Maybe, "Did you happen to see anyone the night of. . . ?" And if he looked guilty or acted the least bit suspicious, well, then they'd know they had a perfect suspect!

Looks Can Be
Deceiving

What do you think, Will?" Katie and Will were walking across the school grounds after lunch the next day. "Is it too crazy an idea?" Will seemed to have recovered from his stomach flu.

"Well, Mike was there while you were gone, that's for sure."

"I hate to be suspecting somebody we know." Katie circled a couple of girls in front of her and came back to Will. "But I feel I ought to do what I can to find Mrs. Stellan's jewelry."

"I know what you mean." Will squinted his blue eyes and looked across the grassy field that was mobbed with kids, as usual.

"Of course, it could have been some real criminal, someone we'd never see again or know anything about," Katie said. "But the police said it looked like a neighborhood job."

"Could be anybody, I guess." Will said. Suddenly he pointed. "Look, there's Mike. Let's go talk to him."

"Okay," Katie agreed but she suddenly felt a little nervous. It wasn't easy . . . trying to find out if somebody was a thief or not.

They ran across the field, dodging in and out of all the games. When they got near Mike they slowed up. At least he wasn't a great big guy. He was actually kind of small, and today he was dressed in jeans and a red jacket and —

"Wait a minute!" Katie exclaimed out loud. She stared. "Will, look at his feet!" Mike was wearing boots, like hiking boots, and they were large. "Will," she whispered, "he has such big feet."

"Oh, man!" Will stared, too. "You're right. They're humungous!"

"If only we could see the bottoms of his shoes."

"I could trip him, then you could tackle him." Will grinned.

How could he make jokes now?

"Will! There he goes!" Mike was running after a soccer ball.

"Let's corner him," Will said.

They hurried toward Mike, who had picked up the ball and was throwing it back into the game. Katie and Will stopped beside him.

"Say . . . uh . . ." Katie began, "could we . . . uh . . . ask you some questions?" How could they do this anyway? Her mouth felt sort of dry.

"Huh? Questions? What kinda questions?" Mike began to back away. Already he looked suspicious.

"Well," Katie licked her lips, "we just want to know — "

"Why do you keep staring at my feet?"

"Because . . . uh . . . they're such great shoes," Katie said quickly.

"Yeah, the greatest," Will put in. "Could I get a better look at them? I have to get some new ones. I just happened to notice yours just now when we were walking by. They look really good for . . . uh . . . hiking and games and stuff."

"Yeah?" Mike looked surprised. "You like 'em?"

"I sure do." Will stared at them as if they were the best shoes he'd ever seen.

"They're really super." Katie stared at the brown, scruffy boots, trying to believe what she was saying.

Mike shrugged, but he looked somewhat pleased. "Yeah? Well, they do the job. They get me there."

"How're the soles?" Will asked, squatting down to get a better look.

"I dunno." Mike lifted his foot in the air and looked inquiringly at it.

"They look like good ones, really thick." Katie bent forward. The sole was grooved and in a pattern and . . . Katie almost choked . . . the grooves formed a U-shape!

But Mike hopped away and put his foot down. "Hey, I have to go now. I'm in that game over there."

"Wait! Don't you deliver papers on Apple

Street?" Katie asked, trying desperately to keep him there.

"Yeah." He started edging away.

"Do you remember last Saturday night?" She watched Mike's face closely. "Last Saturday night," she repeated.

"Sure, what about it?" Mike was backing away, looking around nervously. "Look, I have to go." A crowd of kids came pushing past them, and Mike ducked and ran off.

"Will!" Katie exploded, turning to him. "What do you think? You saw that U-shape on the sole?"

Will grinned at her. "A great suspect!"

"Wasn't that something . . . really something?" Katie couldn't get over it. "Didn't he act guilty when we began to talk about delivering the paper and all that? Oh, Will, and his shoes — do you suppose he did it?"

It was hard to believe, but they seemed to have a perfect suspect.

"Thanks, Will," Katie said as they started back across the school grounds. The bell was ringing for the start of afternoon classes. Katie gave Will a grateful smile. She was just about to ask him what he thought they should do about Mike when someone called him.

"Wil-l-l-l." Out of the crowd of kids swarming toward the school building, Michelle came running toward them.

"Wait," she called, "wait. I want to ask you something."

Katie felt awkward just standing there. Will had looked back at Michelle and now she was in front of him, laughing, talking, pushing back her dark hair. Katie heard her say something like, "I hope so. Oh, try to, Will." Katie hurried away, determined not to look back at Will and Michelle again. Still, she couldn't help wondering what it was all about. What was Will supposed to try to do?

Katie was still thinking about Will and Michelle that afternoon when she was bicycling up and down Apple Street. She had decided to talk to Mike again when he came to deliver the newspapers. She wasn't sure just what she'd ask him, though. It wasn't easy questioning a suspect.

Apple Street was quiet. The older boys were at a football game. Will was on his paper route. No one was around. The maple trees looked bare against a cloudy, gray sky. That last rain had knocked off most of the leaves. Katie passed the Stellans' house and went on down to the corner. She was almost tempted to go around the block to see what was happening on Michelle's street. But why bother to find out? Michelle would probably be unfriendly, and who needed that? Too bad Sarah Lou and Jody couldn't come over on their bikes. But it was a long ride. They were probably doing something together though, because they lived so close. Maybe they were at the mall again, or working on their Christmas lists. Katie sighed. No use her making a list. She'd earned only nine dollars so far.

"Katie, Katie, can you stop a minute?" Someone was calling her. Katie wheeled around abruptly. She recognized the slender figure of Mrs. Stellan on the sidewalk in front of her house. Katie waved and started back.

She wondered what Mrs. Stellan wanted. She'd only sat for her that one time since the jewelry was stolen, and that had really been her own idea. No one else had called her.

Mrs. Stellan was smiling as Katie rode up onto the sidewalk and rolled to a stop beside her. That was a good sign anyhow. "Katie, I need a sitter for next Thursday afternoon. Do you think you could help me out after school?"

Katie beamed. "Of course. I'd be glad to. What time would you like me?" Now for sure Mrs. Stellan didn't think she was a thief.

"I think around four. There's a meeting at Annie's nursery school and I don't want to miss it."

"Fine," Katie said. "I'll come a little before four."

"Good. I'm really looking forward to it." Mrs. Stellan looked pleased.

"Is Mr. Stellan still away?" Katie asked,

wondering if Mrs. Stellan had been alone all this time."

"Yes. He's not coming home until next weekend."

"Is there any more news about your jewelry, Mrs. Stellan?" Katie almost hated to bring up the subject.

"No." Mrs. Stellan shook her head. "The police don't offer much hope, either."

Katie felt a terrible urge to tell her about Mike, and how she and Will were tracking down the perfect suspect. But she decided to wait until she had something more definite to report.

"I'm really sorry it happened, just when I was there and everything." Oh no, Katie felt her lips quivering. Why was she getting into all this again?

"I know you are, dear." Mrs. Stellan patted Katie's arm. "Don't worry. It wasn't your fault." Katie wished Mrs. Stellan would tell that to a couple of other people, Michelle for one. "No one was harmed, that's the main thing." She turned to go. "I better go. Annie is alone. I left her watching television. See you next Thursday, Katie."

After Mrs. Stellan disappeared into her house, Katie wheeled her bike down to the curb. As she started to pedal away she saw the Goldbergs' yardman pull up in his old tan pickup truck. He climbed out and started across the Goldbergs' lawn. Of course now he was the Stellans' yardman, too.

Joe was his name, Mrs. Stellan had said. He carried a rake and began to rake the leaves around the house. He had a perfect view into the house from the large front window.

A yardman could get to know a lot about what was going on in a house and what was in it, Katie realized. She stood still, watching him for a minute. She wished she could see the bottoms of his shoes, but she couldn't exactly go up to him and ask to see the soles of his shoes.

Joe straightened up and waved to her. "Hi," he called out.

"Oh . . . uh . . . hi." Katie started guiltily. This was really something. It was getting so she suspected everybody — just everybody. Still, it was hard not to think about him. While he was working at the Goldbergs' he might have noticed things next door, like Mrs. Stellan wearing her jewelry. Or maybe he could hear things . . . like who's going out at night and when.

Katie shook her head. Stop it. She was becoming a horrible person, thinking rotten things about everyone.

She took a deep breath, swung onto her bike, and began to pedal away fast. The only answer would be to find the jewelry.

The Swap Meet

Saturday morning Katie had just finished dressing when she heard Dick's car horn sound impatiently in the driveway. She grabbed her jacket and headed for the front door.

"Bye, Mom," she called.

She had told her family about her plan. Mom and Dad said not to count on finding the jewelry, but Dick had offered to drive her and Will to the swap meet.

"I really appreciate this," Katie said to Dick as she climbed into the front seat where Will was already waiting.

"That's okay." Dick gunned the engine. "Can't think of anything I'd rather do than catch a crook." He was joking, but Katie knew he'd be really glad, too, if the jewelry ever did turn up.

"So we're off, K the D." Will grinned at her. "Katie the Detective, get it?"

"Got it," she laughed. As they started up Apple Street, Katie suddenly felt hopeful even though

Mom and Dad didn't think there was much chance of finding Mrs. Stellan's jewelry.

When they turned the corner, Katie saw Michelle going up Oak Street all by herself. From the way she walked, Katie guessed she wasn't very happy. Katie almost felt sorry for her. She was all alone while Katie was going off on an exciting adventure with Will. It was such a nice day, sunny overhead with the bare branches of the oaks and elms reaching toward a blue sky. As they drove along, she put Michelle out of her mind and thought about what was ahead.

Soon Dick was pulling onto the road alongside Bigby's Field. The swap meet looked immense . . . counters, booths, and tables, and hundreds of people . . . cars, trucks, vans, and motorcycles filled the parking area. When Katie saw it all, she felt almost overwhelmed. It was so big, there were so many people. How could they hope to find anything?

Dick stopped the car. "Good luck, you guys. I'll be back after I do Mom's errands."

"Okay. Thanks, Dick," Katie said as she and Will got out of the car.

"I'll see you at noon," Dick added. "Is that enough time?"

"Yeah, see ya then," Will said.

"Maybe we'll have some good news," Katie added with a little shiver of excitement. Dick drove off and she and Will turned to face the huge mass of tables and booths of the swap meet. "Shall we just start walking?" she said to Will. "Or do you think we ought to go separately?"

"We better split up," Will said.

Katie was almost sorry to go off without him, but she knew it would be faster. They checked their watches and agreed to meet in an hour by the entrance, and took off. Katie passed all kinds of booths — some were selling rugs, curtains, hamburgers, garden equipment, toys, and used books. There was one table filled with little ceramic statues of Santa Claus holding a tennis racquet. Dad liked to play tennis. He would love one of those for Christmas. If only she had more money.

Katie finally came to a table displaying jewelry. Eagerly she stared down at the array of pins and bracelets and rings.

"Lookin' for somethin' special, honey?" a little, lined-faced man asked her.

"Yes," she said. "Something with garnets."

"You mean real garnets? You got that kinda money?"

"No, no," Katie said. "I don't. I'm just asking for my mother. She wants a bargain."

"Well, bargains we got, honey. But no garnets. Now you tell your mother we've got some real nice pearls and diamonds." He pointed to some in a locked case.

"Okay, thank you." Katie hurried away to find some more jewelry. One good thing about this place, she thought, as she passed a stack of lawn chairs, then a pile of auto tires: It did seem like the kind of place thieves might try to sell their stuff.

She had just finished checking two more jewelry booths, when she saw Will running toward her. He dodged through the crowd, around a clump of kids, and came panting up to her.

"Katie, guess who I saw?" Will looked really excited.

"Who, Will?"

"Mike, and guess what? He's carrying a box, real carefully."

The crowd jostled up against them as they stared at each other. "Oh, Will! Do you think he's got the jewelry? Do you think he's here to sell it?"

"I don't know, but let's tail him and find out. He's down this way. Come on." They both began to run. They'd have to keep out of sight, but that would be easy in this crowd. There he was, dark hair, red jacket, easy to follow, and he was carrying a small box very carefully under one arm.

"See him?" Will whispered.

Katie nodded. "It's Mike, all right." She peered through the crowd. "Let's not get too close."

They hung back and followed him as he moved

slowly from booth to booth. He seemed to stop at all kinds of booths — not just jewelry displays.

"Trying to get a good price, maybe," Will whispered.

Mike moved along and stopped at another display. This time he actually opened the box and held it up to show to the woman behind the table. But the woman shook her head.

"Zowee-e-e," Will muttered. "He's trying to sell something for sure." Now Mike was closing the box and starting off again.

"If he's really got Mrs. Stellan's jewelry. . . ." Katie couldn't finish, she felt such a surge of anger.

"Uh oh, where's he gone?" Will shouted. The crowd was thick, and Mike in his red jacket had suddenly vanished.

Katie and Will pushed through the crowd and found a new row of booths and displays branching off to the left and right.

"Oh-h-h," Katie groaned. "Where did he go? We haven't lost him, have we? I'll look down this way, you look that way."

Will nodded and they separated quickly. Katie rushed down one aisle, then back along the next. There were so many people, looking, buying, talking, sauntering. Suddenly she caught a flash of red by one of the booths.

"Will!" Katie shouted through the crowd. "Will!"

She waved her arms and jumped up, hoping he would see her. She started after Mike, just as Will caught up to her.

"You saw him?"

"Yes, there." She pointed. Mike was still carrying the box. "Will, let's go talk to him. Maybe we can find out something that way."

"Good idea," Will agreed. "We could lose him in this place. Maybe we can find out what he's got in that box. I can't figure it out."

They went hurrying after Mike, pushing their way through the mob of people.

"Hi, Mike," Will called out.

Mike turned around and looked surprised. "Oh, hi. It's you guys." He glanced down at his feet. "Did you come to look at my boots again?" He grinned.

"Well, no, uh. . . ," Will said.

Katie couldn't think what to say for a minute, either.

"So what're you doing here?"

"Well, uh. . . ," Katie paused. How could they ask to see what was in the box? "Same thing you are." She tried to smile.

"Yeah?" Mike looked excited. "Where's your stuff?"

Katie glanced toward Will. This was hard, trying to question somebody. She and Will weren't real detectives, just kids trying to quiz another kid.

"Have you got something good in that box?" Will asked quickly.

Mike grinned. "You bet. I just hope I can sell it here. What are you trying to sell?"

"What are *you* trying to sell?" Katie countered.

Mike grinned slyly. "Listen, I don't want to tell. Then everybody — "

Just then a small boy came hurtling through the crowd and crashed right into Mike. As he fell over backward, the box flew out of his hands and landed with a smash on the ground. The lid flipped open and out poured a whole pile of coins. All kinds. Katie could only stare. Old coins!

"Look, Will," she said, starting to laugh.

Will was staring, too, now looking at her and laughing. They had been so wrong, so really wrong.

"Darn that kid!" Mike muttered, getting to his knees and beginning to scoop up the coins. "It's not funny, you guys."

"Yeah, yeah, you're right." Will agreed. "Here, I'll help you."

Katie felt embarrassed, too, for suspecting Mike, and was grateful for the chance to help him. She kneeled down and began to help pick up the coins.

There were old pennies and nickels, and foreign money, too. Katie felt really guilty. The things she'd thought about Mike. She hoped he'd never know. She was relieved, yet disappointed, too. Their only real suspect, their last hope, was gone.

"Thanks, thanks a lot." Mike was back on his feet, his coins all in the box again. He looked at Katie. "Say, Katie, I just want you to know. I don't believe all that stuff I've been hearing about you."

"About me?" Katie echoed, beginning to get a sick feeling in her stomach.

"Yeah. Michelle was telling me how you and the dog found some of that stolen jewelry out in the Stellans' yard. She made it sound sort of weird — "

"It's the truth," Will cut in. "That's what really happened. The thief must have dropped it when he was making his getaway."

Mike shrugged. "Life is full of weird things, isn't it?" He glanced over his shoulder. "Say, it's getting late. I have to go catch my ride home. Thanks, you guys. See you next week."

Mike turned and walked off through the crowd. So he'd gone, their perfect suspect. And now no one looks guilty, except me, Katie thought sadly.

Dressing Up

Katie decided she'd just have to get used to the fact that the jewelry had been stolen and that they'd probably never know who had taken it, or ever get it back. She would have to wait for people to forget about it — if that was possible with Michelle around. As for her Christmas money, well, maybe the Stellans would keep on hiring her. But she doubted if anybody else would.

On Monday Katie was tossing a frisbee back and forth with Sarah Lou at lunchtime when Jody came running toward them. She stopped in front of them and shook back her short hair angrily.

"I just heard the worst, the absolute worst!"

"What, Jody?" they said together.

Jody looked really cross. "It's about Michelle. I was just talking to some kids. She's giving a big birthday party on Thursday."

"With boys?" Sarah Lou asked quickly.

"Yes, with boys." Jody scowled. "And a whole lot of other kids."

"Do you know who?" Katie asked.

"Not us," Jody snapped back. She looked at Sarah Lou. "Of course she doesn't know us all that well, but get this! She's not asking Katie, either. She's going around telling everybody that if she did, something might be missing from her house afterward."

Katie felt as if she'd been hit in the stomach. "Missing?" she cried.

"Well, that is . . . that is just . . . crazy!" Sarah Lou tossed her head angrily.

Katie looked off across the playground full of kids and felt tears sting her eyes. Michelle was never going to let anyone forget about the missing jewelry.

"Why, that's the most rotten, ratty. . . ." Sarah Lou was fuming.

Katie suddenly realized that Michelle had been inviting Will to her birthday party that day they had been checking out Mike's shoes. She'd been asking him if he could come. Would he, when he knew Michelle was saying those things?

"Jody, are you really sure?" Katie asked.

"Yes, and she's telling how you pretended to find jewelry in the backyard."

Katie had learned that from Mike at the swap meet. She let out a sigh. "I wonder why Michelle tries so hard to make me look bad." Katie frowned.

"Probably because *she'd* look bad if you didn't,"

Sarah Lou pointed out. "I mean, someone might think she'd done it. She lives right in back of the Stellans, and you said she and her little sister are there a lot."

"That's right," Jody agreed. "She could have come in and taken the jewelry the night you were there, while you were out front with Annie. Then she dropped some of it running back to her house."

"I don't think so." Katie shook her head. Somehow she found it hard to believe that Michelle, even mean Michelle, had done it. But she wished Michelle would stop going around trying to lay the blame on her!

"Never mind," Sarah Lou said, putting her arm through Katie's. "Why don't you come over to my house on Thursday?"

"Who needs Michelle . . . and her dumb party?" Jody said.

But Katie suddenly remembered and groaned. "Oh, that's the day I have to baby-sit for Mrs. Stellan. I hate to be down there then, so close to Michelle's house."

On Thursday afternoon as she rang the Stellans' doorbell, Katie told herself to forget Michelle's party. Maybe she could pull down the curtains, turn up the TV, and not hear the music and all the kids. She hadn't mentioned the party to Will. She didn't want to admit she hadn't been invited, but she wondered again if he was going.

From inside she could hear Annie running to the door and calling to her. Everything about baby-sitting here would have been great if only. . . .

Annie pulled open the door. Katie stared at her in surprise. "Annie, what're you wearing?"

"I'm a mommy," she beamed. She was wearing an old white satin blouse and a black skirt that hung to her ankles. Behind her Cheri came clumping into the living room on high-heeled shoes. She was wearing a black hat and carrying an old handbag.

"I'm a mommy, too," she said.

"Well, you both look just super." Katie had to laugh and almost forgot for a moment how bad she felt. "Really, you look terrific, just like mommies."

"Hello, Katie." Mrs. Stellan came into the living room. "I promised Cheri's mother I'd keep Cheri while she and Michelle get ready for her birthday party. I hope you don't mind. I'll be back in plenty of time for you to get to the party."

Katie didn't know what to say, but fortunately Mrs. Stellan didn't wait for an answer. She hurried around, picking up her purse, and taking out her car keys. She was wearing a red wool pants suit but no red and gold jewelry, Katie noticed. No jewelry at all, in fact. "Do you mind taking care of Cheri, too, Katie?" Mrs. Stellan was saying. "I'd be glad to pay a little extra."

"No, I can take care of Cheri." What else could she say? That she didn't want to? . . . Let Michelle do it instead of having a party and leaving her out? It didn't seem fair that she should have to take care of Cheri when Michelle would be having fun with Will and all the others.

"Good-bye," Mrs. Stellan called, heading out the back door. "I'll be back by six."

Annie didn't seem to mind at all today that her mother was leaving. "Come see our other clothes," she said, pulling Katie by the hand.

Katie was glad Annie was in such a good mood. She followed the girls into Annie's bedroom where there was a pile of old clothes and jewelry on the bed.

"Katie," Cheri said, picking up her old handbag. "Help me put on my necklace." Katie glanced over at Cheri, who was drawing a long strand of red beads from her old handbag.

They were beautiful beads: red, sparkling, with bits of gold between each bead. Katie gasped. "Cheri, let me see those." She took them from Cheri's outstretched hands. "Oh yes, these are really wonderful!" Katie exclaimed.

"And see all these." Cheri climbed on the bed and began to run her hands through the pile of jewelry there.

"I want a necklace, too, Katie," Annie cried out, trying to pull a string of beads from the tangled heap of jewelry. But Katie was over by the window now, examining the red gleaming necklace. It looked just like the jewelry she'd seen in Mrs. Stellan's red velvet box that night. She went back over to Cheri. "Where did you get these, Cheri?" The little girl glanced up from the bed where she was draping herself with a string of big, glossy black beads.

"From my box of dress-up clothes."

"Where is that now?" Katie asked quickly.

"Over at my house," Cheri said.

"Katie, help me," Annie begged, pulling at the jewelry.

Katie put the necklace on top of the bureau where the little girls couldn't see it. She checked the handbag, but there was nothing else in it. Then she quickly looked through the pile of jewelry on the bed that Annie was struggling with. It looked like old costume jewelry. Some of the necklaces were broken and there were single earrings, and a twisted bracelet.

"Katie, please," Annie begged.

"Sure, Annie." She knelt to help Annie untangle a long strand of green glass beads. But her mind was whirling with ideas. She was sure that necklace was the real thing. What if Cheri had more of it, the rest of it? This was such an exciting thought, she could hardly stay calm.

"Cheri, do you have any more jewelry in your dress-up box?"

"Sure I do. Look at me, Annie." Cheri slid off the bed and began to whirl around, spinning the black beads.

She had more? Katie felt an absolute chill sweep over her. She had to see that box. Had to. Right now.

"Kids, let's go over to Cheri's. I'd like to see the rest of the things in your dress-up box, Cheri." She tried to sound normal, not too excited. What if Cheri said no?

Cheri put her tiny feet into the high-heeled shoes and began to clump around. "I don't want to go home. I like it here with Annie."

"We'll take Annie. Come on. Let's all go. We can show your mom how nice you look."

It took some persuading, but finally Katie got the girls out in the backyard, in their beads and purses, and headed for Michelle's backyard. Scratch ran along with them. As she opened the back gate and herded them into Cheri's yard, she thought about how hard it would be to have to face Michelle. No way was she going to tell Michelle her suspicions. Maybe Michelle's mom would come to the door instead.

As they approached the enclosed porch on the back of the house, Katie could see the birthday decorations. There were lots of balloons and crepe-paper streamers hanging all around the porch, and a big birthday card was tacked on the screen door. But who cared? Katie had to find out about the box of clothes.

Cheri pulled open the back door. Katie didn't think she ought to just barge in, so she waited by the door.

"Cheri, go ask if we can see your box of dress-up clothes!"

"Okay. I'll go get it." Cheri ran into the house shouting, "Mom, Mom."

When she came back out to the porch, Michelle was following her. Michelle looked surprised, maybe a little embarrassed. "Uh, hi," she said.

"Hi, Michelle. We — uh — just wanted some more of the old clothes the girls are dressing up in." She wasn't about to tell Michelle that she thought Cheri might have Mrs. Stellan's jewelry. What if she turned out to be wrong again?

Cheri grabbed Michelle's arm. "Where's my box of dress-up clothes, Michelle? I need my dress-up clothes."

"Oh, no," Michelle groaned. "Why did she have to ask for them now?"

"Where is it, Michelle?" Cheri was almost in tears. "Where's Mom?"

"Look, Cheri. Mom gave them to the rummage sale at the church. She's gone out to pick up the birthday cake."

"I want my dress-up clothes!" Cheri screamed.

"They're at the church?" Katie shouted.

Michelle nodded. "Mom took them there this morning. Wouldn't you know I'd have to be here just when Cheri finds out." Michelle looked exasperated, pushing her bangs off her forehead.

"Have they had the sale yet?" Katie asked over Cheri's screams.

"I don't know." Michelle shrugged. "But Cheri can't expect to keep all those old clothes."

"What church is it?" Katie was beginning to feel frantic. What if the sale had been this afternoon?

"Get my clothes, get my clothes!" Cheri screamed, all red in the face.

"Hey, Cheri, quit that." Michelle looked up at Katie. "It's the Hemsted Church. Why?"

"Well, look, uh — suppose I go down there and bring back just a few of the things. It's not that far." That was where her family went to church.

Katie kneeled down in front of the sobbing Cheri. "Listen, Cheri. I have an idea. I'll go down to the church and look around. Want me to?"

Her words seemed to get through to Cheri. She broke off crying. "You go . . . get my box?"

Michelle looked relieved. "Hey, yeah. Katie'll go get it." She leaned over and whispered to Katie, "You don't really have to go, of course."

"No, I really will," Katie said. "Can I leave Annie here?" If Michelle knew it was Katie who had started this whole thing about wanting to see the box of clothes, she would be really mad.

"Good, good." Cheri was hopping around now, her face still all wet with tears, and Annie began to jump around, too. Scratch joined them, leaping and barking.

"Okay, I guess. I can keep both of them till Mom gets back." Michelle sounded sort of unwilling as she glanced around at the party decorations.

"I'll leave Mrs. Stellan a note and I'll hurry back. I'll get Dick to take me down in his car." She knew Mrs. Stellan wouldn't mind if the idea ticking away in the back of her head was right. She had to go — right away!

"Well, okay. Just ask for the Purdy boxes."

Maybe it was a wild shot on her part. But she had to see those boxes.

She dashed back to the Stellans' house, put Scratch in the backyard, and left a note on the kitchen table for Mrs. Stellan. She just wrote she'd gone to get Cheri's box of dress-up clothes and had left Annie over at the Purdys'. If her wild idea turned out right, then Mrs. Stellan would be so glad!

Katie ran up the street to her house. But when she got there the house was locked, the garage, empty. They were all out! What rotten luck. Dick must have taken Mom and the baby and Jamie shopping.

She glanced up and down the street. It was deserted! There was no one around. Will was still off on his newspaper route and it wasn't time for Dad to be home yet.

Without wasting a minute, Katie ran to the garage and got her bike. She started up the street, pedaling fast. She'd have to hurry. It was going to be dark soon.

Super Sleuth

A s Katie started off it was already turning dark. Even though her bike had good reflectors on it, Dad didn't like her to be out on it after dark. She'd better hurry. She just hoped they hadn't had the rummage sale yet. If they had. . . . Katie groaned out loud.

But suppose the church was closed? And if it was open would she be able to find Mrs. Purdy's boxes? Katie shivered. Was it from the cold or from excitement? That red necklace looked so real, so like the bracelet!

Katie turned the corner and pedaled past Oak Street. She wished she'd meet Will coming back from his newspaper route. Katie gripped the handlebars hard, feeling again that shiver of excitement. The traffic was getting heavier and the streetlights were on. It was turning colder, too. The chilly air blew right through her jacket and jeans. She wished she had on her gloves and scarf. And she wished she had someone with her, like Will or Sarah Lou, or that she was in Dick's car.

Beyond the curve she saw the low stone wall of the cemetery. She was getting closer and pedaled faster. At last the Hemsted Church loomed up tall and white behind bare tree branches. Now, if only someone was there! She should have tried to call first to see if anyone would answer. Oh dumb-dumb, she should have thought of that, but she was in such a hurry.

Katie skidded across the pebbled drive and wheeled up to the church door marked "office." The windows were dark, but she jumped off her bike and ran over to the door and banged on it anyway. Nobody answered. Pushing her bike along, she started around the church, but every door she knocked on remained silent. The only noise was her feet crunching over the pebbly driveway.

Katie steered her bike around the back of the building and headed across the north side of the church, where the parking lot stretched out — a flat, empty square in the early twilight. No, not quite empty. There was one car in the parking lot. Just as she saw it, she heard a door close behind her. Katie whirled around. "What're you doing out here?" a woman's voice called.

Katie recognized the heavy-set lady on the church steps. It was Mrs. Millard, the secretary of the church. Katie felt weak with relief. "What're you up to, young lady?" Mrs. Millard was quite old and always called the girls young ladies.

"It's me, Mrs. Millard. Katie Hart. I'm so glad you're still here. I have to find something." Katie's voice trembled a little. "Some old clothes that were for a rummage sale."

"Oh, it's you, Katie Hart. I couldn't make out who you were in the darkness. You gave me quite a start. What is it you want?"

"Some old clothes, Mrs. Millard. You haven't had the rummage sale yet, have you?"

"No, not yet." Mrs. Millard slowly descended the steps. "The ladies have been bringing in things all afternoon. The sale starts tomorrow at noon, sharp. What can I do for you?"

Katie wheeled her bike over toward Mrs. Millard and propped it against the railing on the steps.

"Well, I need something from the Purdys' box. They're our new neighbors, you know. There's something in their box they, uh, don't want sold after all. It's a real emergency." No use explaining. Mrs. Millard would probably tell her to go home and leave the Purdys' boxes alone.

To her joy, Mrs. Millard said, "Well, all right, Katie. Come this way. I can take a few more minutes to let you look." She pulled a huge bunch of keys from her purse and went back up the steps to the door. In a moment she had it unlocked and had snapped on a bright light in the hall and another on the basement stairs.

"I'm afraid there's a whole lot of clothes down there, Katie. I don't know how you're going to find anything."

"Are the boxes labeled?" Katie followed the bulky figure of Mrs. Millard in her heavy, dark coat down the hall, then down some bare wooden stairs, and into the basement corridor. It was all brightly lighted now.

"I don't rightly know. The ladies took care of it themselves this afternoon." At the end of the hall Mrs. Millard threw open a door, snapped on another light, revealing boxes of clothes all over the floor. "They're planning to sort everything tomorrow morning and get it all ready for the sale. Whose box did you say you're looking for? Maybe I can help. You start at the end of the room, Katie, and I'll look here."

The two of them began to search, bending over the boxes, checking for labels on the boxes or on the garments inside. None said Purdy.

"How's your family, Katie?" Mrs. Millard asked.

"They're just fine, Mrs. Millard." As Katie hurried from box to box she told Mrs. Millard all about Peter, how he made little cooing noises when she talked to him, and how he could almost roll over, how he loved to stare at his own little hand —

anything to keep Mrs. Millard from thinking about leaving.

Mrs. Millard kept saying, "Yes, yes, that's just the way my Harold used to do."

But in spite of all the talking, Mrs. Millard was soon straightening up and glancing at her watch. "I'm afraid I'll have to go, Katie." She frowned. "I've got to start fixing supper."

"I'll be really fast," Katie promised. "There are just a few more boxes." She rushed from carton to carton, plunging her hands into all the clothes, sifting through the jackets and sweaters and skirts, all the while looking for things that were small and shiny and hard.

But Mrs. Millard was standing impatiently by the door now. "Think you better give up, Katie," she called out. "I really have to go. Maybe Mrs. Purdy could come back herself tomorrow morning."

Katie couldn't bear to call it quits. She didn't dare explain how she couldn't tell Mrs. Purdy her wild idea, either.

"Please, Mrs. Millard, there are only a few more boxes. I'll whiz through them really fast. Just this last row here. It's really important." She rummaged quickly through the next box and the next.

Mrs. Millard was frowning now. "I promised to make a pumpkin pie for our supper tonight." Katie fell to her knees to tackle another box. It would be so easy to miss things in these piles of clothes.

And then she found it — the box belonging to the Purdys! There was an old pink sweater with a name tag on it, "Michelle Purdy."

Mrs. Millard rattled the door knob noisily. "It takes quite a while to make supper."

But Katie wasn't listening. Her tired fingers had closed on something hard. She pulled out a tangle of clothes, and the coronet, the headband that Mrs. Stellan had described, fell to the floor. The garnets and diamond bits sparkled and winked and gleamed in the bright overhead lights.

"This is it!" Katie shouted. "I found it. I found it!" She dove back into the mound of clothes, sifting carefully with her fingers. Yes, there was the choker of garnets and pearls on black velvet . . . and what else? . . . earrings. She had to keep looking . . . yes, two of them, gold hearts covered with garnets. And here was a gold and garnet pin.

By this time Mrs. Millard was standing over her. "Good. You've found what you want." She smiled at the sight of the jewelry in Katie's hands. "That little girl didn't like her mother giving away her junk jewelry, I guess."

Katie couldn't explain now, but she'd come back one day and tell Mrs. Millard the whole story. She hastily gathered up the jewelry and a scarf to wrap it in. And, wait, she must take something for Cheri, who was expecting to get her dress-up clothes back.

"That junk jewelry can sure look good sometimes, can't it? You can hardly tell it from real nowadays."

"Oh, yes." Katie seized a silk print blouse for Cheri, and holding the scarf-wrapped jewels carefully, stood up.

"Let's go, Katie." Mrs. Millard was hurrying to the door. "You got all your things now?"

"Yes. Thank you." Katie thought she had all the jewelry from the way Mrs. Stellan had described it. If not, Mrs. Stellan could come back in the morning. Katie hurried after Mrs. Millard.

They went out of the room, up the corridor, up the stairs, turning off the lights as they went. Katie was so excited she hardly knew what to do. She couldn't believe her good fortune. She felt as if she were floating on air, she was so happy.

"Thank you, again. Oh, thank you," she babbled. "I'll just go get my bike and — "

"No, no, Katie. It's too dark. You let me put you and your bike into my car here. It'll fit in the trunk, I know. I'll drop you off on my way. Let's see, you're out on Apple Street, aren't you?"

"Are you sure that wouldn't be too much trouble?" Actually, it sounded like a wonderful idea.

"No trouble. It's on my way. Now, let's get your bike. Sure glad that little girl will be happy now."

If only Mrs. Millard knew. Lots of people were

going to be very happy. But there was no use trying to explain all this now.

In a minute the bike was loaded into the car and they were driving past the stone wall of the cemetery and on toward Apple Street.

"You and me,
Katie."

As they drove back up Elm, under the streetlights, lights and shadows darted in and out of the car; Katie clutched the bundle on her lap, longing to open it, take another peek, but now was not the time. At least it was a quick drive by car. And in a few minutes Mrs. Millard was saying, "There's Apple Street ahead now."

Katie felt a tremendous shiver of anticipation sweep through her. Now she could show Mrs. Stellan the jewelry! She was too happy, too way up high, to try to figure out how Cheri had gotten the jewelry. But one thing she did know: She had to take it to Mrs. Stellan right away.

"Which house, Katie?" Mrs. Millard asked, turning down the wide, quiet street. It, too, was lined with rows of yellow streetlights.

"This one." Katie pointed through the darkness toward the Stellans' small white house. She must show the jewelry to Mrs. Stellan and make sure it really was hers. That was the first thing to do. But it had to be hers. It was so like the bracelet Scratch had found in the yard, and the necklace Cheri had pulled out of her old handbag. Katie cradled the precious bundle of jewelry in her hands. She longed to go home to tell Mom and Dad that she'd found the jewelry and see the happiness on their faces and hear Dad say, "Katie, that was smart thinking on your part." But first she had to tell Mrs. Stellan.

"Right here," she said. "This little white house."

Mrs. Millard pulled up in front of the Stellans', where the lights were on now.

"Thank you very, very much. I hope I didn't make you too late," Katie said, climbing out.

"That's all right." Mrs. Millard eased herself out of the car and together they went around to the trunk and lifted out the bike. "I'm glad you found what you wanted. Sometimes folks are too quick to give things away."

Katie couldn't take time to explain now. But she made a promise to herself to tell Mrs. Millard the whole story this weekend. Katie tucked the scarf bundle in the crook of her arm and started to wheel her bike toward the curb. "Thanks again," she called and hurried up the front walk. Dropping her bike on the grass, she ran up the front steps. But when she rang the bell nothing happened, except that Scratch barked out in the backyard. She rang again and waited, cold with excitement. Where were they?

Katie leaned against the front door, thinking for a moment. When Mrs. Stellan got home she must've found the note, so then she'd go over to Michelle's. Of course, to get Annie. That's where they were.

Katie darted down the driveway, unfastened the gate, and ran into the backyard. Scratch jumped all over her. "Good dog. Gotta go, Scratch." She ran to the rear fence and through the gate into Michelle's yard.

The party was going on now. The porch was a huge glow of color in the dark night. It was packed with kids, and music and laughter drifted from it.

She ran toward the house. Never mind that she wasn't invited. She was going there anyhow. She had to find Mrs. Stellan. She hoped Michelle wouldn't answer the door.

Katie ran around to the front of the house and up to the front door. A bunch of red and yellow balloons was fastened to the door. Katie rang the bell, still clutching the bundle of jewelry carefully. In a moment the door opened. What a relief! It wasn't Michelle.

"Mrs. Purdy?" Katie asked. "Is Mrs. Stellan here? I have to see her."

"Yes. Are you Katie? Mrs. Stellan's been

wondering where you were. She didn't understand why you had to leave so suddenly." The tone of her voice sounded pretty curious, like, "Why did you leave and where have you been?"

"I'm sorry, but you see, Cheri — " The slender figure of Mrs. Stellan appeared behind Mrs. Purdy. "Katie!" she exclaimed. "Where in the world have you been?"

"Mrs. Stellan. Look! Look what I found!" Katie shoved the bundle at her. "I went to the church to look through the rummage. . . ." She was so excited she hardly knew where to begin her story.

"What?" Mrs. Purdy exclaimed. "What rummage? Come inside, Katie."

Katie stepped into the living room and held out her hands, displaying the jewelry in the scarf, the red and gold gleaming and twinkling in the light.

There was total silence. Katie raised her eyes anxiously to Mrs. Stellan's face. "Is it yours, Mrs. Stellan? Is this your jewelry?"

"Yes! Yes, it is!" Mrs. Stellan sounded flabbergasted. She picked up the coronet, the choker, the heart-shaped earrings, the pin. "Yes, it's all mine, my grandmother's lovely jewelry. Katie, where did you find it?" Mrs. Stellan's voice trembled and she gathered Katie into her arms. "Where did you find it?" she repeated.

Katie looked over Mrs. Stellan's shoulder at the circle of faces. The whole party seemed to have moved into the living room and they were all staring. There was a whole bunch of kids from school, and Will was there, too.

"Where did you find it?" Mrs. Stellan asked again, letting go of Katie and staring into her face. Mrs. Stellan's brown eyes were large and warm and happy.

"Oh, it's so fantastic! You wouldn't believe it! I found it in the Purdys' box of old clothes down at the church."

"I can't believe it!" Mrs. Stellan stared at Katie in amazement.

Michelle, pushing forward into the circle, said in a sarcastic voice, "Yeah, me neither."

"In our box at the church?" Mrs. Purdy asked.

"But — how — why?" Mrs. Stellan broke off, frowning.

"Cheri had the necklace in the old handbag she brought over to your house. She said she had more in her box of dress-up clothes. But when we came over Michelle said the box went to the church rummage sale. So I rode down to the church on my bike. I was afraid they might have sold it. Mrs. Millard showed me the boxes and helped me look through them. When I found a sweater of Michelle's in one of the boxes, I knew I had the right box."

Suddenly Katie remembered the silk blouse she had stuffed inside her jacket for Cheri. She pulled it out and handed it to Mrs. Purdy.

"Yes, that was in the box of clothes I was letting Cheri play with." Mrs. Purdy frowned.

"But how did the Stellans' jewelry get into our box of old clothes?" Michelle demanded.

Katie wasn't sure but she had worked out a possible solution.

"Did you find my clothes, Katie?" Cheri pushed her way into the circle. She spotted the jewelry Mrs. Stellan was holding. "My pretty jewelry," she squealed. "Mine." She reached for them as they dangled from Mrs. Stellan's hands.

"Cheri," her mother said, "why do you think those are yours?"

"Mine," she beamed. "I found them . . . in Annie's house."

"Where?" Her mother looked aghast.

"In a pretty red box."

"And then what?" her mom said sharply.

"I put them in my bag. And I brung them home. And I put them in my box of dress-up clothes."

"Cheri!" Her mother looked stricken.

Katie was thinking fast now, her mind whirling. "I see how it happened," she burst out. "She must have come in that night when Annie and I were out front."

"Good heavens!" Mrs. Stellan exclaimed. "This could all be my fault. Let me explain. One day I let the girls play with some old costume jewelry

121

of mine and I said something about giving it to them later. It was on my dressing table right near my red velvet jewelry case."

Michelle had been standing quietly all this time. "You mean Cheri did it?" Her voice sounded strange and embarrassed, and her face was getting all red and strained looking. "My sister did it?" she repeated.

Will edged forward. "Hey, that's why you found the bracelet in the backyard, Katie. Cheri must've dropped it on her way home. That's got to be it."

Katie couldn't stop looking at Michelle. She wanted to say, "I told you I didn't do it. I told you Scratch and I found the bracelet. I told you. . . ."

But standing near her was Mike. Mike with just the right boots to fit the footprint, with just the right suspicious way of acting, and the mysterious box at the swap meet! It was hard not to make mistakes, she had to admit. And she remembered how her friends had said that Michelle probably took it. But, of course, they only said it because they were angry.

Everyone began to talk at once. Mrs. Purdy was busily apologizing to Mrs. Stellan. Cheri was happily struggling into the blouse. Mrs. Stellan was cradling her jewelry in her hands and looking around at everyone and smiling and didn't seem to be blaming anyone.

Then Michelle came up to Katie. "Would you like some punch and cake?" she asked. Her voice sounded so eager, as if, maybe, she was offering more than just punch and cake.

"Thank you," Katie said. She suddenly realized she was both hungry and thirsty.

Michelle darted away and returned in a minute with chocolate cake on a paper plate and a cup of red punch.

"I wish you'd stay," Michelle added, her face flushing under her dark bangs. "I mean, I know you have your own friends — but maybe just for a little while?"

"Well, uh. . . ." Katie was so surprised. Michelle was asking her to stay? She could see the embarrassment still in Michelle's face. Katie took a sip of the punch, not bothering to talk, just enjoying the cool, delicious drink.

Michelle spoke up again, "You know, it's hard to be new. Everybody else already has friends." Her dark eyes looked so pleading now. It really surprised Katie.

"I have to go home now," Katie said. She had to tell her family the good news. And after she told them, she wanted to call her friends.

"I wish you'd come back," Michelle urged.

"Maybe I will." Katie turned to leave.

"Hey, Katie, where are you going?" Will called.

"Katie the big D! How'd you get so smart anyhow? And without my help?"

Katie laughed and pulled open the front door. "It just happened, I guess."

"I was wondering where you were." Will followed her out the front door. "You're the only reason I came."

Katie turned to look at him in the brightly lighted doorway. Waves of surprise and pleasure washed over her as she realized he wasn't kidding! They stepped out into the night together, closing the door behind them.

"Katie, I've got a surprise for you." Will took one of her hands and dropped something into it. She looked down. In the dim light from the streetlamp she saw a shiny toy badge. She held it up. It said "Super Detective" on it.

"Fantastic!" she laughed.

Will grinned back at her. "You and me . . . we'd make a great team, don't you think?"

"Great!" She beamed at him. "Thanks for everything, Will." She pinned the badge on her jacket and looked at him. "You're right," she laughed. "We would make a good team."